Lich Ears

C.K. Malavasic

Published by C.K. Malavasic, 2024.

Also by C.K. Malavasic

Siren's Score
Containment Web
Lich Ears

Watch for more at https://ckmalavasic.com.

Table of Contents

Acknowledgments

For the two family members who will never read this work yet encouraged it, the many family and friends who will enjoy once it's published, and those amazing readers who will join in on this adventure.

Lake Death

Crags & Spires

Unlivable

Spire of Defeat

Sjoret

Ihovet

Laeb West

Onlae

Free Tradezzone

Trader's Last Stand

Laeb East

Wulae

Mol'Ava

Slaider

Dy'Wanei

L'pitth

Darksteel Keep

Nevon

Lich Encounter
Z. Yowar's Path
Major City
Country Boundary
Alarm Boundary

Prologue

Life

Her first memory was of voices and being wrapped in softness.

"Her eyes," a concerned male voice worried.

"When she's older we can replace them with clearer gems. She'll have to make do with opaque black ones," a calm female voice preceded a touch scrapping on her head, "She's our love made real. We'll make sure she knows how precious she is to us."

But that love and care wasn't to last.

Fearful people invaded her home, attacked her family.

Then they shattered the bones of her parents, cursing them to never cross to the other side, for being different. Only because they were monsters of death.

She survived by huddling in the small space between the walls, listening to them break her life apart.

Heard their glee in finding the artifacts her mother collected from far off places, and her father guarded rigorously.

Hunger and cold meant nothing to her as she fearfully shivered in the space, saying nothing even hours after their voices faded into the distance.

When she crawled out, sought out her family, felt the shards of bone which cradled her with so much love and care, she realized one thing.

Never would she get to see the world her parents promised her.

Chapter 1

Scorching Funeral

"Alone with only armor covering us"
Heat tried to warm her, but nothing could touch the ice coating her spirit.

She could feel the sun on her armor, warming until it felt like a fire. The ground creaked and cracked as the moisture evaporated underfoot, her booted steps louder for the accompaniment of the earth crying out as it dried.

The scent of dry grass breaking under her boots joined with the taste of dust which threatened to cling forever to her mouth.

Voices reached her as she approached the priest and grave diggers, or she assumed they were based on their voices, the sharp clink of metal on dry, hard ground and incense used only during a funeral growing more pungent the closer she got to them.

She could hear where the hole descended into the earth, the final resting place of her last friend.

A voice urgently whispered, "The Black Knight. He's really here."

Another hissed, "Be silent. He'll kill you. He's not like the Blue Knight we are burying today. She'd have given you a nod and a kind word."

She stopped on the side of the mourners, wondering why no others stood with her.

A bell tolled in the distance, once, twice, then a third time.

The priest's voice trembled for a moment then slowly firmed up, "We are gathered to send one of our own on her way to those wardens of death on the other side. Bearing her armaments and cherished items, with her dearest family and friends at her side, we consign her to the earth from which the food she ate rose from. If any wish to speak of her life, speak now."

She spoke softly, her baritone voice resonating in the helm and beyond, "Of those she met, she inspired to greater aspirations than those grounded by fate. She dared to be a knight of the realm when others scoffed at her. When no one would ride with her, she found those who would. To protect the weak with her shield, and lay low the wicked with her sword."

Kneeling, she bowed her head, "Honor, dignity and fortitude follow you to the other side, my friend."

The priest stammered, "Will any others speak?"

Only the wind answered for a minute.

"With the words spoken, may she be guided to the other side and her final rest. From earth to sky and back, we fulfill the cycle."

The sound of metal digging through soil preceded the dulled thunk of dirt hitting wood.

Each shovelful sent her friend further from her, until she knelt at the filled in grave.

"We leave the family and friends to stand watch until morning."

The priest and grave diggers walked away.

She stayed kneeling, unmoving as the sun's warmth left her, cold seeping in to steal the day's heat.

She prayed her friend would not rise.

She didn't want one more to be crushed until their final rest claimed them for the other side.

Keeping her vigil, the scents of dry ground changing to the chilly bite of night, she waited.

He walked towards the gravelands, resisting the jaunty tune in his head as he used the paths between the hills to hide his approach from any watchers.

A knight had been buried today. One with mighty fine armor and weapons.

They would fetch him a pretty bit of silver. Maybe a gold piece if he was fortunate.

Climbing the hill hiding the gravelands from the village, he froze when his head peeked high enough to look into the valley.

The moonlight highlighted the grave as a wound on the otherwise arid landscape.

And the armored figure kneeling beside it.

A friend of the knight?

How could that be?

The Blue Knight should have been the last of her group.

Except the dark armor at the side of the grave bespoke the truth.

Pausing, he considered the unmoving figure.

Normally there were at least a dozen family and friends to hold vigil over the deceased, allowing each to take a shift while others rested.

This one was alone.

He just needed to wait for sleep to claim them.

Crouching down, he smiled.

It was the last thing he did.

Chapter 2

Necromancer's Folly

"We march towards the horizon"

Her head lifted as an all too familiar cry echoed off the hills. It called her to arms in defense of the body deep in the ground.

Standing smoothly, she drew her spiked mace and sledge hammer, using her ears to locate the befouled creature.

Wingbeats drew closer, the sound of them indicating a sizable creature. One of the biggest she'd faced of this creature's kin.

"Upon this ground," she began chanting, "the wind will assail those air borne, bucking all from its back."

The air around her swirled, twisting faster and faster as it grew in height.

The creature squawked in alarm as a howling gale challenged it.

This was the only time she could know her surroundings in a way similar to sight. Or at least as close to it per how Grella once described it to her.

When her magic encountered magic of another individual, she gathered details as if directly touched, tasted, or smelled.

Faint pressure as if her hands stroked with her wind magic outlined the creature in the air, as the taste of old leather filled her mouth followed by the bitterness of preservation liquids. Long dried flesh with a hint of rot encompassed her.

The creature's wings struggled to keep it aloft, beating furiously, yet finding no purchase against the tornado running wild around it.

Then her tornado vanished, her magic canceled out entirely. A dispelling spell of a fairly high level.

"Clever," a voice spoke from a hill opposite her, "Most would burn it rather than take away its aerial advantage."

Wingbeats faded slightly, still audible. A vibration began to grow stronger, felt through her boots easily.

"You are not taking this knight from her well-earned rest," she stated calmly.

"What would one knight do against all of my creatures?"

Before she could respond, a young voice challenged, "You face more than a knight, necromancer."

"Oh, a sidhe of the Winter Court? I feel nothing... but laughter," cackles filled the air.

Locating the newcomer, she fretted at their proximity to the hill where the enemy stood.

Normally she didn't reveal her non-trivial spells in front of others. However, this enemy may require her to invoke them shortly.

Moans began to fill the air along with the clatter of bone.

Carcasses and skeletons marched their way to the grave.

The winged horror above cried out and was answered by at least a dozen others.

The winter sidhe barked a word which instantly dropped the temperature and added the scent of impending snow.

"Cold does nothing to my minions. Pity you didn't mind the knight there."

A swear word from the Winter sidhe made her want to sigh.

She inhaled though she didn't need to breathe as she prepared the one thing that would end this fight quickly. One which would mark her as other, yet again.

A lower level spell of one she learned long ago.

Her bellow echoed over the hills, "Break your bonds and return to the other side!"

Siolobha, Guard of the Winter Court, gaped as the winged horrors fell from the air as soon as the knight gave the command, crumbling as they descended until only dust drifted down.

The necromancer looked equally stunned as he turned, gasping as he noted all his creations collapsed, dissolved or turned into rotting piles.

Siolobha stared at the Black Knight, standing with weapons readied for combat. A sentence, a command was all he needed to end an undead army.

Who was he?

The necromancer's next words worried Siolobha, "I see now. You are a fellow necromancer. If I had known, I would have left this fallen knight to you."

"You have come to the wrong conclusion," the Black Knight rumbled darkly.

"Come now. A powerful knight like the one lying under your feet is well worth the time to turn into an undead."

The snarled counter seared Siolobha as if she were bound in a summer-scorched hot spring, "This knight will not rise again."

The agony and anger in the tone made her shiver.

"Pity. I will have the knight," a flash of sickly green light lanced at the Black Knight before she could call a warning.

Except the Black Knight dodged it as if it was a thrown rock.

Siolobha notched an arrow, fired at the necromancer.

Only for it to be deflected by a large sword.

The air shimmered in front of the necromancer and a ghostly figure appeared.

A wraith warrior?

Her arrows couldn't harm a wraith as they were untouched by cold.

Only a Summer sidhe's arrow could dispel it.

Swearing under her breath she drew another arrow, hoping to distract the wraith her way so the Black Knight could engage the necromancer.

She fired.

Then gaped as her arrow changed from an icicle to a heat image of an arrow.

It struck the wraith, which issued a banshee like cry before vanishing.

Siolobha glanced at her black ice quiver, then her frost encrusted bow.

How could she have fired a summer arrow without damaging her bow?

"Who are you!"

Glancing at the necromancer, she jerked.

The Black Knight towered over the necromancer.

"The vigil keeper of the knight while she makes her way to the other side."

The sickening crunch made Siolobha flinch.

Even the frost giants couldn't make such a noise with their great mauls.

The Black Knight turned away from the crushed body, moved swiftly back the grave side.

Then to her surprise, knelt.

As a true vigil keeper on watch would.

Swallowing, Siolobha approached cautiously.

When the Black Knight made no moves, just knelt with mace and sledge hammer on display, she crouched, resting her bow across her knees.

The silence stretched out, filled with tension.

"I can keep the watch next," she offered hesitantly.

"You were her friend?"

Siolobha bowed her head, "She saved the life of the King of Winter when my youth and inexperience failed him. I owe her more than I can repay, so watching over her on this final day is the least I can do."

"Then we both will keep the watch," the Black Knight stated, bowing his helm in respect to the dead.

Scanning the horizon, the moonlight helping with distance, she pondered the skills of the Black Knight.

A spell which dropped undead as if he was the creator of them. Then the way he climbed the hill in an instant. His strength in wielding a sledge hammer in one hand when most used two to heft one marked him as extraordinary.

How did the Black Knight acquire so much power, and within a human lifetime?

The Blue Knight, Grella Harth, honorary member of the Winter Court, was alone when she saved the King's life.

She said she rode solo, her fellow knights long dead.

Yet how was this Black Knight around?

The Blue Knight spoke the truth, bound by the magic of the court, yet this one obviously still lived.

"May I ask why the Blue Knight said all her fellows were dead? Did she not know you lived?"

The Black Knight didn't reply.

Siolobha looked down at the ground. Flinched.

She uttered the word to remove her spell bringing a piece of winter to this land.

"Please forgive my forgetfulness," she flushed in embarrassment.

"For what?"

She stared at the Black Knight in surprise, "For bringing winter here long past the danger was extinguished."

Frost decorated the edges of his armor as the air warmed slowly.

Then she noticed no icicles dripped from the mouth guard.

Only those of winter and the undead wouldn't leave the evidence of warmth quarreling against cold.

He turned his helm, "What has alarmed you?"

"There are no icicles on your mouth guard. I know you are not Winter Court."

The Black Knight sighed, breath blowing snow into the air.

Snow which didn't melt from his breath.

"It doesn't matter if you know, Sidhe of the Winter Court."

The helm came off and the sight beneath made Siolobha stare in shock.

The gemmed eyes which should be sparkling clear sat dull and pitch black as the skull turned to her. The jaw moved as words captured her full attention.

"I am Z'ronia and I'm a lich. It's why she would say all her knights are dead. Though, I never was alive."

"What?"

"My parents were both liches. Somehow their love produced me, though with flaws."

"Flaws?" the world spun around her.

"I'm blind," the helm slid back into place, "Now you know why Grella told you such an odd truth."

She sat back on her butt, her breaths coming fast, "Why haven't you...?"

"If your question pertains to desecrating the body of my friend to make her undead, I will be severely cross with you."

Flinching at the fairly mild rebuke despite the phrasing, she got back to kneeling, "I thought liches were evil and created undead at will. Was that a tall tale?"

"I wish it was," the Black Knight, no, Z'ronia replied with bitterness, "But all I've met are that way, with the exception of my parents."

Siolobha opened her mouth to ask about his parents, then paused as two things shook her mind nearly to pieces.

He spoke of his parents in the past tense, as in dead. Suggesting permanently dead rather than just undead, which may be a sore subject.

The second pertained to the name Z'ronia: it would only be given to female offspring.

Chapter 3

Insights on Humanity

"Flushing out enemies with our hollow shells"

Z'ronia listened for more dangers, half berating herself on revealing her nature to a sidhe of the Winter Court, half exhausted of loneliness.

Grella asked her three decades before to leave the kingdom lest she be discovered as undead. Not just any common type of undead, but the worst kind: A lich.

No matter how honorable she acted, no matter how loyal her spirit declared itself, she'd be hunted down and destroyed.

Humans feared all strange and unnatural beings. They would chase the sidhe holding vigil with her as much as her if they came across them.

Grella tried to find knights to serve as her brothers and sisters in arms but had been rejected by normal ones.

Then she sought those to elevate instead of be discouraged. Grella found her first.

Z'ronia couldn't tell how much time passed since her parents were killed, but it felt like eternity.

Even the shards of their bodies disintegrated long before Grella entered her home.

The strange sound echoing in her home alerted her to something moving beyond stray rodents.

She climbed the walls, then hid in an alcove high above the floor.

She outgrew her previous hiding place at some point, so she used the alcove as her new bed and resting place when she wanted to let her mind drift.

Steps, metal on stone grew louder, along with the strange crackling those who killed her parents brought with them.

Sitting silently, hoping the fiends would leave again, she waited.

A voice broke the tension, "A reliquary?"

Z'ronia held perfectly still, scared to move as the steps paced about below.

"The fools," the voice continued, "Relic Guardians were the most sacrificing of us all. No wonder they have vanished. Hmm?"

Rocks scrapped on rocks, almost like the noises her father produced opening one of the hidden safes, making Z'ronia tense more and more the longer the sounds came.

Then her chest filled with warmth, as if her parents nuzzled her once more.

A sob escaped her before she clutched her mouth to muffle the noise.

"Relic Guardian? You shouldn't keep your soul jar where enemies can find it."

Z'ronia shivered, fighting the grief welling up in her.

"Alright. I'll leave your soul jar on the table. You should collect it and carry it with you. I'm sorry to disturb you."

The sharpness of the cold made her curl in on herself, the missing warmth leaving her suddenly bereft.

The steps departed, fading quickly.

Z'ronia waited a time, then carefully climbed to the floor.

The sounds echoed differently, a sign of how much had been moved and changed in such a short time.

Moving silently, she approached the only surface which counted as a table any more.

She patted the top tentatively.

It took several minutes until she touched something different.

A metal container.

Gingerly picking it up, she explored the surface, twitching as certain touches sent odd sensations through her.

Soul jar?

What was a soul jar? Why would it be hidden? Why carry it?

Clutching it, she climbed back to her hiding place, confused and frightened.

Struggling with what memories she could remember of her parents and their lessons, she tried to piece together some understanding.

She recalled her father describing the items he guarded relics. So the strange person's comment about Relic Guardians made a little sense, when the word order was changed.

Guardians. Plural.

Her mother. They both must have been Relic Guardians.

Which meant she was supposed to be one, too.

Was this soul jar her first relic?

How did one guard a relic?

How could they guard a relic when others would destroy the guardians?

Her mind tumbled from thought to thought, lost in what it all could mean.

"The knight proved useful for something after all. We don't have to worry about any undead in here," a voice pierced the silence.

Z'ronia stilled, clutching her relic close to her chest.

A second voice scoffed, "Did we need to worry? All I see is rocks, dust and these two rusted jars."

Jars?

Like the one she held?

Something clanked as it hit rocks. A sound she recalled making when she stepped near the entrance and brushed something on the floor with her foot.

"See nothing to fear in here," first voice sounded disappointed.

Second voice hummed, "I bet the knight took anything worth collecting. That gives me an idea."

The first voice purred with a nasty undertone, "Are you thinking of killing the knight and taking all her stuff, including what she found here?"

"Yeah. Let's go," the second laughed, "the knight won't know what hit her."

Z'ronia listened as their footsteps faded away.

What did it all mean?

Was a relic taken from here by the person who spoke of soul jars?

Who were the other two? Why did they want to kill a knight?

A knight was a guardian. Her mother spoke of them as fellow travelers doing similar tasks, just defending in different ways.

The first one, the soul jar speaker, must be the knight.

She climbed down the wall, then quietly moved through the corridors, stepping carefully in case anything else shifted since the last time she traveled through the halls.

Coming to the archway she couldn't pass through, she paused.

She heard nothing.

How could she warn the knight she was hunted?

This was the edge of where she could wander.

An enraged bellow jolted her.

She turned and ran back to her alcove, climbing as fast as she could to reach safety.

Crouching down she shook as yells, clangs, and other noises drew closer.

Like the terrible sounds those who killed her parents made.

Curling over her relic, she trembled.

"Getting tired, knight?" one of the two bad voices taunted. The one who broke the silence first.

The soul jar speaker, the knight taunted, "Takes two of you to wear me down? Seems like you tire easily."

Second voice snickered, "All that armor has to be heavy."

A clang made Z'ronia shake uncontrollably.

It was happening again.

The horrid memories of her parents last moments overlaid the fight going on below her hiding spot.

"I wear heavier armor so this set feels light," the knight challenged, "Unlike you who can handle leathers only."

Grunts and clangs scuffled back and forth below.

Then the clang of rock on metal.

"Pin her," the first voice ordered.

"Can't do anything now, knight," second voice chuckled, "Without the skeleton here, we can have our fun."

Z'ronia hated the awful two voices below.

If only the rocks would drive them off.

A rumble grew in the room.

"What the?"

Rocks hitting rocks and metal filled the room, drowning all other sounds for several long seconds.

Then the noise began to die.

A strange taste filled the air when the rocks stopped shifting.

Metallic.

Like the copper coin she once bit as a child. Her father chided her, saying coins were worth trading as long as they didn't have bite marks on them.

The knight's voice rose up, "Appreciate the help, Relic Guardian. I owe you one."

Twitching, Z'ronia asked tentatively, "Help?"

"That spell was pretty impressive without using a chant," a groan echoed, "I could have done without the beating, but at least they're dead."

"Dead?" Z'ronia shivered in horror, "I killed them?"

"I doubt even a necromancer could put them back together again," a grunt along with foot steps, "Would you come out of hiding? I'd like to thank you properly."

Feeling sick at having ended a life, even those as vile as the two speaking before, she crept to the edge of her alcove.

"Hello, Relic Guardian. I'm the Blue Knight, Grella Harth."

"Blue?" Z'ronia cocked her head.

"The color of my armor, at least when it's not covered in dust like now. It's more tan at the moment."

She puzzled over the statement. Her parents never described anything as blue or tan. They used textures, tastes, sounds, scents, but never those words.

Sight, she reasoned out, could be where blue or tan fit since they never used colors before.

"Are you alright? You seem to be looking at a wall."

Z'ronia jerked, unsure what to say.

Grella inhaled sharply, "You're blind, aren't you?"

Cowering back into safety, Z'ronia shook.

"I don't mean any offense, Relic Guardian."

"Not Relic Guardian," Z'ronia knew she couldn't defend a relic, not even the soul jar she held.

"Then what are you?"

"Z'ronia," she offered hesitantly.

"The midnight bloom."

"Midnight bloom?" She moved back to the edge of the alcove.

"Z'ronia means midnight bloom. It was once the name of a noble house that has long since fallen to ruin. The last descendants died out half a millennium back."

"My parents named me after their friend who died long ago," she replied sadly.

"Parents?"

"They were the Relic Guardians. Until the people came and killed them," Z'ronia huddled around her relic.

The silence echoed with tension, until Grella asked, "When did this occur?"

"I don't know. Long ago."

There was a scratch of metal on metal, "The villagers near here are not the sort to respect you are a Relic Guardian. It's best you leave before they get too brave."

"I can't leave. The archway down there is as far as I can go."

"Which archway?" Grella asked.

Z'ronia climbed down hesitantly, clinging to the soul jar even when she stood on the floor, "This way."

Grella paced beside her, moving at her speed as she shuffled along the corridor to the archway.

"This one," she stated softly.

"Liches are limited to sixty feet from their soul jar, or so the ancient scrolls say. This is nearly three hundred feet," Grella sighed, "The Relic Guardians and liches are supposedly born from the same set of spells, but this discrepancy is interesting."

"Limited to sixty feet?" Z'ronia asked.

"Your soul jar, the one you're carrying contains your soul, your spirit. What makes you, you. If the jar is destroyed, you would be destroyed with it."

Z'ronia touched the relic in her hands, "This is me?"

A soft sigh sounded, "Unless there's another Relic Guardian back there, this is your soul jar. Since it's with you, you can leave. You can travel anywhere you want with it by your side."

Cross the archway?

Travel like mother used to do to collect relics for father.

Shaking in terror and hope, she stepped forward.

Pass the archway.

"My camp is outside the cavern. Hopefully my horse didn't bolt," Grella stepped ahead, her boots sounding on the floor.

"Horse?"

Grella led her outside, the first time Z'ronia had ever heard it, much less stepped on the soft unsettling ground.

Z'ronia pulled from her memories as a creature lowed in the distance.

A corpse hunter.

"This vigil will be difficult," Z'ronia stood up, sighing.

"What do you mean?" The sidhe of the Winter Court asked.

"Corpse hunter," Z'ronia shook her head, "The really nasty necromancers and mages use those beasts."

"Are they vulnerable to cold?" Siolobha asked, looking up at Z'ronia.

"No. Nor fire. Drowning works, but no water here and the magic to summon enough to drown it would be exhausting. You just have to beat them down or use weapons enchanted by masters until they don't rise again."

Uttering a swear word which turned into snow a few inches from her mouth, Siolobha notched an arrow, "I am ill equipped for this."

"Is this your first vigil watch?"

"Second. First was trivial in comparison," Siolobha scanned for the enemy, her eyes sweeping sky, ground and areas between.

"Cold from the depths, untouched by summer, rise to shatter others with icy disdain," the words sent shivers down Siolobha's spine.

The ground cracked, split in front of Z'ronia, parting for a handle.

The bone white haft was wrapped with gray leather as it rose from the earth.

Then the head of the weapon pushed out of the ground, mist floating from it as it made contact with the warmer air.

A war pick.

One formed of a piece of winter.

Z'ronia hefted the weapon, spun it around.

To hold out the handle to Siolobha.

"This is yours. I would not take such a weapon from you," she backed away.

"No, it is yours. Arrows will do nothing to what comes. Save them for who commands the corpse hunter," the reply spoken with conviction, "Besides, I can tell you didn't bring more than a knife as a secondary weapon."

"How can you tell?"

"The smell of metal chilled with frigid clear water at its forging, lighter scent than a sword made in the same manner. Mink oil in the leather wrapping not only your bow but another weapon. You would have drawn it if it had the reach, yes?"

"I wouldn't have been able to tell from such small signs," Siolobha frowned, putting her bow away.

"Without sight, I must rely on my other senses. Such small signs are enough to give me forewarning of danger. Please take this war pick. You'll need it to face the creature thundering our way."

"I hear no thunder," Siolobha gripped the handle, surprised at how it felt in her hand.

As if made for her.

"Allow me to impart wisdom to you," Z'ronia held out a hand, dangling a chime on a chain.

She lowered the chime, barely letting it rest on the ground, the chain taunt.

Siolobha heard the ringing clearly, growing louder.

She'd seen one of the older guards drop to the ground and listen early in her training, then call out a warning of a raiding party.

"Sound doesn't carry well through the ground and you aren't close to hear it," Siolobha hurriedly clutched the chain Z'ronia released into her hand.

"Hold it just enough for the chime to rest on the ground and you'll know your answer."

Siolobha did as instructed, then blinked at the vibrations crossing her skin.

She looked at the metal boots Z'ronia wore, "You feel it."

"Keep the chime. It will serve you better than me."

Quickly packing it into a pouch, she asked, "Can you tell how many approach?"

"At least two corpse hunters, though only one has sounded its presence. The second is smaller, more likely an ambush type. They are masking their owner's steps, assuming he or she is walking after them."

Siolobha pointed, "There."

Then flushed with embarrassment, forgetting her companion was blind.

"Speak towards the direction you see them," Z'ronia suggested.

She did, then Z'ronia gave a sigh of relief, "Then I can do something I haven't since I left Grella and her company."

A large inhale of air proceeded a single word of such complexity Siolobha couldn't comprehend even a thousandth of it.

She understood the results when the land shuddered into a gaping chasm, the figure running towards them on six legs lowing in alarm as it fell, the ground it used suddenly dropping.

Then the dirt clapped back together with clashing force, burying the corpse hunter deeper than the knight they guarded.

"Is it dead?" She asked.

"Yes. The rocks would have ended it, grinding it as grain to flour beneath a mill."

Siolobha kept the observation to herself Z'ronia could rival one of the court mages with such magic. Only her blindness restrained her from a position in any court who'd have her. Assuming, they welcomed her at all.

She turned, then yelped, swinging the war pick.

As if guided by magic, the point of the pick punched through the skull of the creature, just behind its empty eye socket.

Its weight crashed on her, pinning her to the ground as she struggled to get out of its embrace.

Only for it to crack apart, going to pieces above her.

Standing shakily, she stared at the weapon in her hand.

"No weapon of mine should be able to make anything brittle with winter's bite. How?"

Z'ronia's tone saddened, "My speciality is crafting items. Only a few I have memorized and can do without sighted helpers or asking for magic to give form to it."

"You are giving me this for nothing?"

Z'ronia's voice carried a hint of smile, "We are both holding this vigil, yes?"

Before she could reply, flames exploded into a raging, swirling tower, bathing the area in baleful red and orange light.

Heat buffeted her, making her cough from the dryness.

As if summer reached out and swatted her.

A strange voice called out a challenge in a foreign language, filling all the air with its power.

Z'ronia countered in the same language, her weapons held at her side.

Out of the flames stepped a figure.

Horned and clawed, it snarled as it gestured to the grave.

A demonic mage.

Siolobha heard of them, whispered in hushed tones even among the hardened warriors of the Winter Court.

The least among them would stand tall even against the King of Winter filled with power where his season held dominion.

LICH EARS

Then she remembered what Z'ronia stated earlier. She turned her head and yelled, "This way!"

Chapter 4

Parting

"Booted feet drumming our dreaded path ahead"
Z'ronia would have smiled if she possessed lips.

While the sidhe lacked experience like that of an older warrior, she possessed the adaptability of youth.

Z'ronia could aim her spell.

Incanting the binding circle so it rested on the air in a limited area, she invoked the greatest threat to a mage bearing demon blood: a mage bearing blood of their opposite yet more powerful element.

The air stilled before the silence took on a strange echoing quality.

Z'ronia hated bringing a mage of this sort to her since it stripped her of her primary sense, yet she would do anything for Grella.

Even allow herself to be destroyed to protect Grella's remains.

"You dare invite a lesser one against me?" The demonic mage challenged.

"No one said I called a lesser one," she countered softly.

She couldn't use this spell more than once every fifty years. Not for lack of power, but out of courtesy.

For a brief moment as her magic crossed with the one coming at her spell, her senses knew every dry blade of grass, the taste of air, dirt and the chilled skin of the sidhe beside her, every scent in the area and where it emanated from etched into her. Extending for what felt like to the edge of forever, she knew even the details of the demonic mage.

Then she felt a rumble beneath her, filling her with details of the earth and stone deep into the ground.

She tasted and felt the angelic mage appear in front of the grave.

Then nothing as her magic finished its work.

The noises of battle were brief, seconds only.

Ending with a gurgle of a fatally destroyed throat.

Blazing heat from the demonic mage vanished, replaced by the watery tranquility of the angelic mage.

"You've kept your word well for one of the undead," the voice lilted with kindness and solidarity.

Z'ronia wanted to sigh at the subtle jab but buried it, "Of course. I would not wish to anger you nor your tower."

A tense silence stretched between them.

The angelic mage blew out a breath, "Grella said not to judge you as your brethren."

Z'ronia turned her head to the grave, grieving for her friend who'd reach the other side shortly, "I'm grateful for such a friend and will be long past her memory is forgotten but for me."

"This...this is her final resting place?"

Z'ronia bowed her head, her voice thickening with her pain and emotion, "Yes."

A huff of breath, "You may call on me again. This one time we will count as outside our agreement."

"I will honor our bargain," Z'ronia started to argue.

"No," the firm word shattered her resistance, "You asked for her, not yourself. Consider it payment for her services which cannot be repaid in any other way now."

Z'ronia lowered her head further, "As you wish."

"Let us close out the vigil so she may travel to the other side," the grass crackled as someone sat on it, "I pity any more who dare attempt to grave rob this night."

Z'ronia moved back to her position, knelt.

The Sidhe of the Winter Court rejoined her, nervously shifting her weight.

"You speak demonic, angelic. How did you manage this?"

"Grella would read to me," Z'ronia spoke softly, "when she could gain entry to libraries for research. I cannot write the languages, but I can speak them and understand what is said."

"Shouldn't demonic words summon a demon mage?"

Shaking her head slightly, Z'ronia corrected, "As itself, the language cannot conjure up anything, just as any language used to chant spells. It requires intention and power to make it more than pretty sounds drifting through the air."

They stayed silent a long time after that, only a wind playing with the grass keeping them company.

Z'ronia felt a shift in the ground.

The reaching grasp of the other side stretching through the earth, moving with purpose to Grella's remains.

Grella once described the instant the spirit of the departed joined the other side as the spirit gripping the forearm of the hand of the other side as they were beckoned onward.

Z'ronia shivered as contact was made between the Grasp and Grella, then all those sensations leaving, fading into the distance.

"It is done," clothing sliding against skin sounded as the angelic mage straighten, brushing her clothing with brisk motions which filled the silence, "The vigil is ended with her safe travel to the other side."

Z'ronia nodded, standing as well, reciting the traditional words, "To the ground from all came, she has returned. May we all find such a cycle peacefully when our time comes."

The Sidhe of the Winter Court added, "May the seasons circle through until this grave is no different from all other spots of this world."

The angelic mage departed, taking the sense of water with her.

Dryness assailed them instantly as a gentle warmth caressed her armor.

Z'ronia put her mace and sledge hammer away, then began the march to where her horse was stabled.

"Z'ronia?"

She paused, waited for Siolobha to continue.

"Where will you go?"

"I'll travel as the wind does. Continually onward," Z'ronia felt the emptiness in those words weighing on her shoulders as the missing spots where she once had company lay empty at her sides.

Siolobha looked at the back of the armor, the weary set of Z'ronia's body prompting her like a whip.

"There's a land, far north. A country the courts warn all but the strongest from. Only the rulers and their closest vassals visit there and return safely."

"Why are you telling me this?" Z'ronia asked, the deep voice seeming as tired as her body.

"I've heard rumors only, but those of strange persuasions may find refuge among the citizens. However, if the laws are broken, a dark creature will visit those who have crossed the order, with no regards to nobility, influence nor money. Blood is the price of injustice and sometimes death."

"The name of this land?"

"L'pilth," the words strange on her lips, Siolobha felt better for saying them.

"I haven't travelled north yet. West, east, south, but not north," she stepped then paused, "If you have need of me, call."

"Need?" Siolobha asked.

"If one of yours needs a vigil keeper," Z'ronia held out her gauntleted hand, a smooth rock with tiny glyphs etched on it sitting in the palm, "Toss this into a fire, even a cold one. I will hear it and ride to you."

Siolobha stared at the stone, "You have done more for me than I can ever repay."

"You helped see my dear friend to her well earned rest, against enemies you had no skill against, with a strange ally most would flee from at the drop of a stone. You trusted a weapon given to you and forged a bond with it that will serve you to the end of your days," Z'ronia turned her helm, the slits hiding her dull black gem eyes from prying gazes, "You have proven yourself one I would be glad to assist. Should my weapons or magics help one of yours cross over without interference, I will do all in my power to repay that willingness to fight at my side, with my determination."

She stepped forward, reached out, hesitated, then took the stone, "The Queen of Winter is ailing."

"I hoped that rumor nothing more than a lie," Z'ronia blew out a breath, stray dust blowing in the light of dawn before mingling with the clinging dirt on her armor, "Call and I'll come to you should I be able."

Siolobha stood with a formal posture, "I, Siolobha, youngest of the Court Guards of the Winter Court, will summon you with your stone upon the fire should one of mine need a vigil keeper."

"Siolobha," Z'ronia spoke her name with deep respect, "Fair you well on your way home. May frost glitter in your wake."

Siolobha replied, "May good fortune chase you with each season."

Z'ronia nodded, then started walking towards the village.

Too soon to her, the Black Knight slipped from sight.

Siolobha looked at the grave, whispered, "You played your words well. Pity the King didn't know when you lived. He would have kept you with us."

LICH EARS

She ran lightly across the ground, leaving nothing of her presence but glitter quickly evaporating into mist in the summer sun.

Chapter 5

King's Troubles

"Voices raised in union as banners float above us"
Sliding the game piece up the inner spiral, she sulked, "It wouldn't be so bad if I had a knight to ride my domain during this time of year."

The Queen of Summer laughed, shifting a piece on the outer spiral to a cross path towards the inner spiral, "It can't be that bad, King of L'pilth."

Scowling at the amused queen, she grumbled, shifting another piece distractedly, "The last five knights fled as soon as the mere rumor of what I am reached them. They barely stepped on my land before turning tail and fleeing as if one of your hounds chased them."

"Perhaps it's because of your well kept beard and kingly presence, Rathi. You are a handsome man, even among my court."

Rathi paused stroking her beard, "They didn't get to see me. They left before I heard they were even in my country, much less in sight of my keep."

Rathi had been born with a body of a very lean and fit man, including a healthy beard and mustache which matched her long hair. All man but for her loins.

The body her parents lamented to the day they drove her out for being other.

Shortly thereafter, a vampire's attack froze her in that state, eternally a man in his prime, save for her gender.

30

"Perhaps a compelling offer to ensure they reach your Darksteel Keep?" The Queen chortled at the snit Rathi sent her way, "Oh, come now. You'd get a knight."

"I want an honorable one so I don't get complaints during the days when the sun never sets," she tapped a piece with a finger tip, "Plummet."

The Queen took the piece off, and Rathi set her piece in its place.

"Are you sure there is no deeper reason for today's laments?" The Queen asked moving a piece to the inner spiral.

"I do not need more to fuss over," she countered by sending one of her pieces across the lower tier to the outer spiral.

"You have been without a consort for nearly a year," the Queen made her move then settled back, "Didn't you have any enjoyment from the man?"

"He," she scoffed angrily, moving her piece as if she wanted to throw it, "said it was a nasty pity my dungeon is poor complement to the walls of my keep. That is besides the gossip I am keeping company within the same gender."

"Dungeon complementing the keep walls," the Queen caressed her mouth, then tapped one of Rathi's pieces, "Plummet. I will see if the King of Summer finds that phrase as amusing as I do."

Taking the piece and setting is aside, Rathi put her chin on her fist, glaring at a wall as if it insulted her, "I would give up on complementary dungeons if I could get a....cuddle."

The Queen sat back, "Didn't you try that some time ago?"

"I had to erase their memories of me since my blood-drinking scared them into nervous fits, the weak feminine fools," she moved a piece, gestured to herself, "This wasn't enough to keep them here, nor all the money in my vault from the centuries gathering it. I'm too ghastly to have a welcoming bed and a partner waiting."

The Queen considered the spirals, tilting her head as she reviewed the pieces remaining, "I would offer to whisper in my court, but..."

31

"That would cause a war between the seasons," Rathi finished when she remained silent for several minutes, "As much as I desire companionship of a more intimate nature, I am not giving up my games."

The Queen tapped the top of her spiral, "With all your angst and distraction, you still best me."

Rathi looked at the spirals, slumping in the chair, "Again?"

Resetting the pieces with a smile, the Queen asked, "Do I need to have my game masters create something more difficult than Enemy Walls?"

"I fear if I did that, they'd come out with sun swords and force me to till the fields while weakened. Don't laugh," Rathi admonished, "They did it before. Twice."

"Then let us play a game of the mind then," the Queen settled more comfortably into the chair, "If you could wave your hands, utter a spell word or two, and conjure a solution to either of your problems, what would you desire?"

"Right now? A knight who can handle all the bandits and invaders during the days when it's only daylight outside. If I could have that taken off my shoulders, I'd be a much happier King."

"What would be the skills of this knight? Come with squires? Wield a mighty weapon? Ride a majestic beast who transforms into a wonderful lover of our body type?"

Rathi sent her an incredulous look, "The last can go to your court. Magic. They have to have magic. All but a few of the threats cast the spells themselves or possess items that throw spells."

"Magic. What else would they wield? Any mundane weapons?"

"Crushing or smashing would be best. The constructs are bothersome in the least, terrors in the worst," Rathi slid down in her chair, staring at the ceiling, "Close range, since we hardly get clear sight to do a distant attack. Not with ninety percent of my land being steep cliffs, valleys and sharp bends."

"Tunnels, caves, and other features. Yes, up close and personal does sound like a good fit. How about sure-footed, even in an ice storm?"

"Since this is hypothetical, yes. Must be like a goat up icy paths."

"Maybe able to hold you against those slippery walls while pleasuring you both with experienced hands and body?"

"This is the knight still," Rathi chastised.

"Two for the purchase of one is best when so many run away," the Queen paused, "I am needed elsewhere. We can continue this when I have a moment."

"Take your time. It's not like I don't have all the time in the world with my mortality stripped from me."

Rathi watched the Queen of Summer shimmer like a heat image, then disappear.

Blowing out a breath, she straightened as her seneschal's clopping steps grew closer.

"Pardon the intrusion, my king," The massive horns appeared first as Ghir'ali, the tallest and strongest Minotaur in her employ entered her quarters, "An attack started on our southern border."

Rubbing her face, "I swear each year these attacks worsen."

Ghir'ali snorted, fluttering the feathers adorning his nose rings, "I have my bow and quiver. Shall we meet them?"

Rathi nodded, "Yes, though..."

"I get daylight fights," he gestured with his horns, "Shall we, my king?"

Standing from her seat, she prayed to the elder deities to have a knight sent her way before daylight held sway all day long yet again.

Siolobha walked wearily into the realm her court held dominion over this time of year, the far south lands.

Traveling in lands where her court didn't hold sway proved more exhausting than she planned for.

She made it back only by the grace of her melee weapons.

Z'ronia's war pick proved impervious to summer heat, freezing even fire elementals in one blow.

Siolobha checked she still carried the summoning stone which sat in her pouch.

Only to realize her pouch was gone.

"You need to be more aware, dearie."

She turned and faced her personal bane, Prince of Winter Celion.

He held up her pouch, smirking nastily at her, "Lose something?"

On her way back, she'd picked up a new spell, one she knew she wouldn't have sought out prior to meeting Z'ronia.

Pouring her intent into her words, she summoned her pouch back to her side.

The pouch vanished from Celion's fingers, popped into the air over her hand to land softly in her palm.

"Tch, you befoul your..."

"You learned a spellllll!" Another voice squealed as the court mage, Fab, rushed them, "Happy day! You managed a third level spell in a few short weeks. Oohhh!"

She watched Celion's face darken, "How dare you skip over the darkest night rituals and obtain a weapon outside them."

Fab took up her war pick examining it, "This is not one of ours. Well-crafted and respectful of the seasons call from the core of magic. A master crafter would only make one of these in his lifetime, unless immortal," Fab held out the weapon to her, "Who gifted this to you?"

"The first vigil keeper of Grella Harth," she answered honestly.

"Do we know of this vigil keeper?" the warm voice made Celion's face change to neutral.

Siolobha knelt, "My King."

"Stand my youngest guard," the king's voice mirrored the slightly warmer winds which preceded the worst blizzards, "We wish to know of how the Blue Knight's passage to the other side went."

Her gaze slid to the ailing co-ruler of Winter. Unlike the humans, the Kings and Queens of the seasons were not married to each other, and often times not the same gender as the human titles bestow on them.

The Queens of Winter and Summer were female, the Queens of Spring and Autumn male.

The Queen of Winter bore high color in her cheeks, a sure sign of her losing her winter chills.

Looking back at her King, she inclined her head at his steady gaze.

Unsure how to relay the juxtaposition of Grella's comments and the true identity of Z'ronia, she began, "I arrived at Grella's final village after the start of vigil. A necromancer challenged the first vigil keeper, the Black Knight."

"How is that possible?" The Queen looked around then focused on Siolobha, "Grella told the truth when she declared her company all dead."

It was best to get it over quickly, Siolobha thought as Celion's malicious gaze tore at her.

"The Black Knight is undead."

The King looked positively pleased, "A vampire?"

Blinking at his odd comment, she shook her head, "No, my king."

Celion interrupted, "Then what kind of undead?"

"A lich," she flinched at the gasps around her.

The Queen scowled at the others before asking, "What type of lich?"

"Type?" Celion sputtered, "All liches are evil."

The Queen blew out a breath, looked at the King, "You know, yes?"

"A lich wouldn't normally hold vigil for someone as powerful as Grella," the king twirled his beard, "Grella passed over to the other side, correct?"

"Yes, my king. I saw the heat shimmer of the Grasp's summer form. It took Grella successfully."

"There are three types of liches," the King explained, "The first are indeed the evil ones and most common. They besmirch their honor and spirits with foulness before becoming undead. They are one of the few the demonic and angelic mages must struggle with to overcome in battle. The second kind serve as tomb guardians for deities, set to watch over the corpses of those deities whose bodies need centuries to crumble away. They would change their service to the next deity in need, rarely venturing beyond their strongholds. The third stood as reliquary guardians, entrusted with the most dangerous, vile or sacred relics to be kept safe to the end of time. Some of those would travel to retrieve artifacts stolen or given to their keeping for the first time."

The Queen coughed, her breath misting the air instead of dripping snowflakes, "There is a fourth, though very rare. I've met twelve in my time, compared to thousands of the others."

"What type, my Queen?" Fab asked, "I had only heard of two, the first the king mentioned."

The Queen looked at Siolobha, "Can you guess at the type I refer to, young guard?"

Like the flash of sun light between bouts of snow, she did, "Born from two liches."

The silence stretched a moment, before the Queen smiled with the beauty of fresh snow, "Please confirm this one's name for me."

"The Black Knight's name is Z'ronia."

Relief relaxed the Queen's shoulders as tears streamed partly down her cheeks before freezing, "Thank you Elders for not taking the last of that line."

Celion demanded, "What line?"

The Queen grinned, "Graspers. The one line who'd ensure the dying return to the other side when it's their time without interference. Their eyes show their true nature, icy blue of sky reflecting on frozen lakes."

Siolobha swallowed, "My Queen...she doesn't have gem eyes like that."

"I know," sadness effused the Queen, "Tell them why her eyes will never be those of her mother, instead opaque and black as winter night."

"She's blind," Siolobha felt like a heat image shimmered before her, warning of her death at the hands of summer, "You knew her parents."

"Her mother asked me for a vision. It took most of my strength, some never to recover. She will never be equal to her father nor mother for she'll never see the world like we do."

The Queen departed.

"Blind means weak," Celion stalked off, "It's better the Grasper line has ended for all the good they've done."

Gripping the pouch, the stone digging into her fingers, Siolobha muttered, "No, we need those like her."

The King's hand on hers jolted her.

"The Black Knight gifted you a weapon. Make sure you take care of such a gift. A Grasper's weapon will always bring true death to the undead. Make sure you practice with the Master of Arms so it is an extension of yourself."

Fab held the weapon so she could pick it up, then slide it into the loop at her side.

She opened her mouth, then shut it.

"What is it?"

At the King's soft words she looked where the Queen vanished, "I told her of the lands to the North. I need to..."

"You sent her to King Rathi's lands?" Fab looked at the King, then tapped his lips, "I bet a satchel of my best cold brewed tea, those two fight on first meeting."

The howling laughter from the King countered, "Three casks of my best ales they are like two halves of one whole."

Siolobha blinked, "I don't understand. Isn't that land dangerous?"

The King gestured for her to join him and Fab, "The four kingdoms due south of King Rathi's kingdom kill all strange beings, those of us belonging to the seasons their top prey. King Rathi on the other hand welcomes us all. We only bring our strongest as they can survive the journey and subsequent attacks, even during the height of our season."

"She's blind. They'll kill her."

"If we hadn't heard of her true nature before you, I doubt any human would discover it so easily."

Fab perked, "I wager one tin of my strawberry jam she has an illusion or a spell to distract others from her true nature."

Siolobha followed her King and Fab as they discussed how Z'ronia hid herself so well for so long.

Chapter 6

Traveling

"Snapping leather strands borne high aloft"

She touched the lowered head of her mount, speaking softly, "Is it time, my friend?"

The soft whinny confirmed signs the barding vibrated in ever stronger pulses, overwhelming the jangle Z'ronia used as guide to where her mount stood.

"I hope you enjoyed your adventure. Let's find you your last rider," she patted the horse's barded neck, metal clicking on metal, "There's a village ahead we can review if you don't want to go further."

The nuzzle made her nod.

Taking up the reins, she walked beside her mount.

They never lasted long, but she didn't mind. Grella said letting go meant one path closed while opening a hundred new ones.

Her mount stopped, pulling the reins taunt, huffed.

"Now?" she asked.

A stronger whiny sounded.

"Very well."

She unbuckled the barding with practiced ease, shouldering the pieces easily. As the last piece detached, the jangle silenced.

Then she replaced the enchanted reins with a standard one.

"Better?"

A nuzzle was her reward.

Stepping carefully forward, Z'ronia pondered the unwinding road ahead.

A land with strange beings, the growing rumors whispered.

Ruled by the same king for three hundred years.

King Rathi.

A monster.

Honorable man.

Lover to men and women.

Commanding horned beasts.

Powerful.

A crack of wood splintering drew her to what sounded like a steep ditch.

"Ow," a raspy voice grumbled.

"Are you in need of help?" she inquired as her mount bumped her shoulder.

"A new wagon and a new back," the sound of rough cloth scrapping hard ground preceded stillness, "Just my luck to break my wheel."

Her mount bumped her again.

Z'ronia took the hint, climbing down the incline gracefully.

By the sound of the air around the person and their vehicle, a two wheeled wagon, meant they were in disastrous outcome.

Z'ronia easily lifted the wagon, listening to the threatening creaks, "Do you have a spare wheel?"

"This is the spare," the voice groused.

Whispering the spell Grella helped her perfect, Z'ronia placed her hand on the ground, lifted it gripping a temporary wheel.

"A mage?"

She slotted the wheel, bracing the wagon with her shoulder as she used the handle of her mace to tap a locking pin into the hole.

Easing back, she listened to the wagon settle.

It wouldn't last long, since the wheel would only hold for a week at most, but it would serve.

"The wheel is conjured. It will dissolve back to the soil it came from," she held out her hand, "You are still sitting. Are you injured?"

"Just my pride," the grip on her wrist held strength as the person stood, "My goods on the other hand."

"Let's collect them. I can do minor mending if the damage isn't too severe."

They spent several minutes collecting all the items that tumbled from the wagon when the wheel gave. She hefted the boxes of goods which survived or she could mend, setting them carefully in the wagon.

The shattered items were collected, some with the hope they could be remade in a new form.

"You act differently than the rumors say," the person whispered.

"What do the rumors say about me?" She asked, curious.

"Where the Black Knight rides, the powerful are killed as equally as the powerless. Disrespect is met with torture and suffering, while respect is no certainty of being left alive. Those you like will be caged in magical chains to be turned into monsters."

Z'ronia found the further she travelled from her original kingdom, the more outlandish the rumors became, though the stories north focused more on her supposedly monstrous side.

"I'll keep those in mind," she gestured to her former mount, "Come on, you have work to do."

"What? I couldn't. He's yours!" The person shifted uneasily.

The truth came easily to her, remembering how her current mount met her, "A previous village gave me this one for defeating a lich who took up residence in their abandoned watch tower when my previous mount fell in battle. Unfortunately, he's a nag and not suitable to be my mount. However, hauling a tiny wagon like this is one he's suited for."

Pulling spare bits of leather, Z'ronia fashioned a rudimentary harness by touch alone, tying it as best she could to the wagon arms.

Her mount nuzzled her.

She patted his neck gently, "Slowly forward."

Walking along side both wagon and the person, she moved down the ditch until a gentle slope presented itself.

Once they were back on the road, the person led the way to a nearby village.

Z'ronia didn't mind the silence, having lived with it for so long.

Noise, especially cacophonies, made her twitchy.

She avoided major cities and large towns as best she could.

However, Grella once told her people don't normally remain silent. They talked, chatted, gossiped and yelled.

"May I ask about the upcoming village?"

The person next to her stumbled, but recovered, "Um, what do you want to know?"

"Any threats I should know about? Undead, beasts of abnormal size, highwaymen?"

"No. Or at least I don't think we have any. We are really close to the border of Sla'der. They hunt most supernatural creatures to extinction. Highwaymen don't use this road since the main one further east has wagons on it nearly every hour."

Z'ronia picked this road so she could avoid the wagon trains and the too-interested guards they usually employed.

They made it to the village without issue.

"Gregnar!" A voice called, "Did your wagon break again?"

"Yes, but this mage helped me," the person beside her replied, "I lost some potions though when my wheel cracked. I only got the bottles left."

"I'll take the bottles," a young voice preceded a short individual, most likely a child.

Z'ronia picked up the box with the broken items, handed it to the child who said, "Mama will love these. Thanks mage!"

"What is this wheel made of?" Another voice asked.

"Earth," Z'ronia answered, "It's conjured so it will only last a week, or thereabouts."

Silence spread around her.

"Is that the Black Knight?" A whisper grew into mutters and fearful mumbles.

"Stop that!" Gregnar called out, "The mage helped me. You know how the rumors are about me, right? I'm a murderer. Is that true?"

The child asked, "Are you the Black Knight who rode with the Blue Knight?"

Z'ronia needed to master her grief before she could respond, "I am."

"Any one who rode with the Blue Knight is a champion," the child moved off, yelling, "Mama! Papa! Come see who came to town. It's the Black Knight."

Z'ronia stood answering questions as to the road she travelled, what creatures she fought against and others she had limited knowledge of.

"Is the horse trader in?" Gregnar asked softly, "The Black Knight gave me this horse to help with the wagon and I think he needs a proper mount."

"We haven't seen him for a couple months. We did get that plodder which limped into town a day ago. Should be able to carry the Black Knight."

"Plodder?" Gregnar inquired.

"Looks like left for dead, but escaped the wolves somehow. Bite marks, along with whip scars."

Z'ronia turned her head, "May I meet this plodder and find out if we fit?"

Gregnar chuckled, the scratching of fingers on scalp clear in the air, "You got good ears."

She also had a great sense of smell. Enough to know most of those nearby needed to bathe a smidge more.

Grella insisted her group bathed regularly, or used cleansing spells to ensure they never looked like they'd ridden through mud, grit and blood. Z'ronia agreed those principles should be extended to all people, regardless of their way of life.

At least Z'ronia knew the cleansing spells as easily as she did the spell to cause rocks to attack on her command. Her armor would nearly always be pure black, or whatever color Grella set up when the two of them adjusted the armor spell so many decades ago.

"This way," a voice offered from the crowd, "I got the plodder set up next to my blacksmithing shop."

She followed in her leisurely manner, finding after so many decades among humans if she moved as if relaxed, those around her didn't tense to attack or flee.

The heavy breathing of a large animal preceded her guide stopping and stepping aside, their footsteps grinding on the dirt road, "This is the plodder. Not much to look at."

Z'ronia didn't mind looks.

Only temperament and tolerance proved worthy mounts.

Horses had one of two responses to her: Fear or delight.

Never a middle ground.

Grella found in the texts all Relic Guardians with mounts bore similar experiences. Only those horses who could sense beyond the aura of death to the loyal soul within could buck the fear.

A long moment stretched in silence as the breathing turned to snorting and pawing the ground.

Then a trumpeting cry broke the stillness, the horse thundering her way, heavy set hoof beats speaking to its weight and height.

Delight in its every action.

Z'ronia held up her hand, then patted the forehead which bumped her gauntlet.

She spoke so lowly only she and her new mount could hear, "Well met, my friend."

A whinny, then a head-butt to her shoulder, strong enough a regular human would have been on their ass in the dirt.

"The plodder never reacted to us like that."

"Horses are very smart. Treat them fairly and they will bear you into the core of the other side, then return with you. How much?"

"How much?"

"For the plodder," she clarified, "I would compensate you fairly for such a companion."

"We don't have any good use for a plodder nor one with a limp."

Z'ronia opened her money pouch, instantly casting the spell to tell her the material the coins she touched were forged from.

Pulling ten silvers, after verifying through touch the faces of the coins were correct to the country the villagers belong to, she presented them, "Would this suffice?"

"That's a full harvest's worth of money and far more than the plodder is to us."

Z'ronia held out her gauntlet, "Then for the plodder and enough grain to get us to the next village. The rest is for the next caravan who treads this way."

"If I refuse, would that insult you?"

"No, but you may discover the coins later with no idea how they got there," she replied with amusement.

"Come over to the store house. We'll get your grain."

Z'ronia spoke softly to her new mount, "Stay here. I'll be back for you, my friend."

The neigh trailed her to the storehouse.

Rathi scowled down the canyons from each part of herself, the differently colored owls she'd broken up into easily scouring the land for enemies.

She relished the days of almost endless night.

Drifting on the air, she watched the ground for enemies, eyes piercing the deepest shadows without effort.

It was a pity the only thing she spotted turned out to be allies. She wanted to drain some enemies dry and hang their corpses somewhere visible.

Swooping down, all her parts gathering together, she watched the mounted warriors riding ahead of the main column, searching for enemies.

The Winter Court's frost-themed weapons glistened with additional power being in their season brought them.

A new guard graced the caravan this time, a young one if Rathi's eyes did not betray her.

The King of the Winter Court halted, lifting his head so his hood fell back, revealing his vigor and health.

Sickness caught Rathi's attention the next instant.

She paused, then turned all her large eyes on the Queen of the Winter Court.

Ailing even to her vision, the Queen coughed weakly as the carriage brought her into Rathi's kingdom.

Gathering all her pieces into one flock, Rathi soared down, merging the pieces until she set foot on the ground.

"Welcome to my kingdom, Winter Court," she greeted warmly.

The King bowed his head with respect, "We are glad to find ourselves here with little issue, King Rathi."

Rathi nodded, then frowned as the Queen struggled to rise from the carriage.

She offered her shoulder and arm to the weary Queen, who gratefully took them both to rise.

The Queen's once strong voice sounded raspy, "I appreciate the graciousness of your welcome, King Rathi."

Pecking a kiss on both of Rathi's cheeks, she eased herself back down with an exhausted sigh.

"I'm sure my chefs will be happy to serve a grand meal on your arrival to my keep," Rathi bowed before stepping backwards.

To have her gaze land on the new guard again.

With a weapon which belonged to a much older guard.

"Our new addition is Siolobha, one of our youngest Royal Guards," the King gave brief smile to Rathi, "When we are seated at your gracious table, we will have one of the growing strengths protecting us all."

Rathi read between the lines.

The young guard proved her mettle in wielding the weapon and thus could be trusted to grow into a more important position, like an icicle from the roof of a cavern.

"I will extend my normal visitor rights to your latest addition," Rathi turned, scowling, "If you'll excuse me. It seems some enemies desire my attention."

Splitting into her owl flock, she swooped up and over the tops of the canyon, her sharp hearing detecting the clacks of a village alarm.

With grace and speed she arrived at the village.

Her eyes spotted the multi-legged constructs first, their glistening crystal hides drawing her in.

She hated the constructs most of all among the enemies who invaded her lands.

They had no blood for her to recover expended energy nor aid her in healing from wounds they dealt.

Diving from different directions, she cursed the lands to the south for being such monstrous cretins.

Her country did nothing to them but exist.

Each set of talons scored the eyes of the constructs, her wings carrying her flock to a space where she reformed.

All the enemies whirled towards her, leaving the village walls alone, at least for now.

"Crystal again?" She sneered, knowing from prior encounters those controlling the constructs could hear her, and answer if they so inclined.

Today being one they were inclined to speak.

"Abomination," several voices hissed as one.

"Coming from you who must be sacrificing hundreds of commoners to build your constructs, that is a compliment," Rathi snorted, "My citizens need not fear their king."

The constructs leapt at her, mandibles gaping wide.

Dodging agilely aside from each, she drew her weighted saber, slashing with it instead of her fingers.

She didn't need to chip another nail on these enemies since she knew from experience her saber proved a more efficient weapon.

Limbs and mandibles separated from the bodies, her movements without waste.

She turned after slicing the last mandible, surprised how frail these constructs were, "Seems the blood and spirit of your people are weakening. These didn't last even half the time the previous set did."

The voice hissed, "You will not always be in power, abomination. We will kill you."

"You'll kill your own country long before my throne is vacant," Rathi snorted as the construct crumbled, the magic being reclaimed to its makers.

With the distance the magic would travel, there wouldn't be much left.

Yet the enemy always chose to reclaim than to release. As if they needed every wisp of magic back.

Rathi considered her words may be closer to truth than she intended. Perhaps they'd murdered so many of their own they were scrapping the bottom of the barrel for remnants.

"My king?"

Looking up at the watch tower and the watchmen there, Rathi cocked her head.

"Those went down much faster than before, your majesty. Are we sure they are weakening and not sparing for something worse?" The grizzled man asked.

Rathi looked at the crystal powder, "Crystal has been their best one yet. I can't imagine what they could use that would top it," she petted her beard, "Would this powder be of use to one of our trade partners?"

"We'll collect it, but most likely will be like the previous times where they want no part of it, your majesty."

"See if the craftsmen can use it for something. Waste not what the enemy provides," she flew up, breaking into her owl forms, one splitting off for her keep, the rest continuing their patrol.

The one arrived and hovered near her seneschal.

"The Court of Winter will be arriving shortly. Provide their comfort while I'm detained."

The nose ring feathers fluttered at the snort, "The usual?"

Rathi considered, then stated, "Ensure the chillest quarters for the Queen of Winter, along with a personal attendant."

"Rumors true?" Ghir'ali rumbled unhappily.

"Unfortunately," Rathi heard another village alert, "Seems tonight will be busy. Ensure our local bards are adequately supplied so they can entertain until I arrive back."

"It will be done," Ghir'ali moved inside the keep, closing the door.

Rathi whirled to engaged the next enemy.

When she returned in the wee hours of the morning, she fought the frown on her face.

All four kingdoms sent in raiders this evening. At least some of them could be drained and left as warnings. Sparkling powder wouldn't deter other interlopers like a bloodless corpse.

Ghir'ali met her at the door to the hall, "The bards will welcome a lengthy break."

Nodding, Rathi waited for Ghir'ali to open the doors and announce her, "Rathi, King of L'pilth."

The air felt icy on her skin as she strode into the hall, snowflakes drifting down from the rafters.

The King of the Winter Court raised a glass, "Would you like to partake of some blizzard ale? This year's harvest is delectable."

"I will," Rathi swept over to claim a glass, noting the Winter Queen slept near the ice brazier Rathi kept on hand for wounded guards of the Winter Court.

Sipping, she paused, running her tongue over her lips to gather the bits of ice the ale left behind.

Savoring the flavor, knowing she had no warmth to ruin the taste, she nodded politely, "This may best the one you brought two centuries ago."

"Both have their strengths," the King of the Winter Court settled more into his chair, "How fairs your border?"

"As it normally is this time of year. Was your crossing impacted by anything interesting?"

"No one hampered us. The cold here is more frigid than norm for this season. I have the impression most huddled in their cottages rather than be foraging in the winds."

Rathi settled on her chair, "I wouldn't be surprised if we get a blizzard or two in the coming weeks. It would slow down three of the four encroaching on my lands."

"True. I doubt anything but the end of days to stop all four."

"That, or an army of mages who'd take their constructs down with a word."

Rathi noticed the new guard reacted, but settled quickly.

Curious, but not rude, Rathi returned her attention to the King, lowering her voice so the Queen wouldn't be disturbed, "I'm sad to see the rumors are true."

The King nodded as the Queen's consort draped a blanket made of snow onto the Queen's slumbering form, "It will not be an easy fight when the time comes."

Rathi swirled the ale, dreary thoughts plaguing her, "Do you have enough allies when it arrives?"

"Not as many as I would like. The seers are almost to the last disturbed. It will come down to two or three choices which lead to victory or bitter defeat."

"Do you know which choices determine it?" Rathi asked softly.

"They say it will be in the middle of the battle. Honor and loyalty will make or break her return to the other side."

Rathi blinked, considering the sleeping Queen, "She has not been able to scry more?"

"She says it will come down to a single spell which will swing her fate, either to servitude or passage."

Rathi sipped the ale, then offered, "If you need me, I will answer your call."

"I fear we will need all our allies to get to that moment. We'll ensure there is a spell to bring you to us should we need you."

Nodding, Rathi nodded to the game board Ghir'ali carried in, "Would you care for our usual bout?"

The King nodded, "I would. Best of three for starters?"

Rathi grinned, "Are all your guards betting this time?"

"Are yours?"

They laughed as Ghir'ali set down the board and began setting up the individual levels.

Chapter 7

Crossing

"Our weapons gleaming with our intent"

She didn't like this country, and neither did her new mount as they traveled the road to the next village.

Something was deeply wrong with it.

Z'ronia didn't know what exactly disturbed her senses and her mount couldn't tell her his thoughts on the matter, save to toss his head nervously.

Plodder, her mount, trotted through as fast as he could, the barding removing his limp and returning his stamina.

The first village seemed normal, bustling with townspeople who initially closed with her until something drove them back to their stalls with murmured unease. The confused-sounding children snatched inside before doors slammed shut moments before she could pass.

Upon reaching the second village, she heard less voices belonging to the young or old. Less slamming doors and more fear in the voices.

The one she last passed through echoed with misery-filled tones. Voices belonging only to adults, most sounding hale and healthy, but for the despair.

Even the woods they passed through, though it was heading into spring, felt empty. As if no birds nor small animals ventured out into the open, not even to nibble on the first grasses she could smell in the chill air.

Since she could not see, she often had to rely on a directional spell to help her stay on a path going the right way.

She was getting closer to the area where north felt stronger than any other direction.

However, each step closer made her more tense.

As if something lingered on this side.

She pulled the reins on Plodder, feeling his surprise to be halting so soon in the day.

"Stay here a moment," she ordered, dismounting.

Listening to the snow crunching underfoot, the scent of winter losing its hold on the land filling her helm, she stepped over to a tree creaking under the weight of snow.

Kneeling, she brushed aside ice-crusted snow, feeling wetness seeping into her gauntlets, along with cold, though neither bothered her.

When she reached dirt, she placed her palm on it, casting a spell with a brief thought.

She recoiled, standing with alarm.

The Grasp of the other side scratched at the underside of the earth, as if it urgently tried to reclaim what was its right to collect.

A lich resided nearby. Not a good one, based on the feeling from the ground.

One who'd lived here a long while to cause the Grasp to become so aggressive.

Yet, she heard not one rumor of a lich being this far north. They preferred warmer climes where the villages became vivacious towns or cities filled with people, or along major trade routes, those that were not closed due to snow for weeks or months.

It could also be the lich muted rumors to keep its presence here unknown but for the malady of the villages nearest it.

However, liches in her experience preferred to collect the healthy villagers for their armies. Yet the villages nearest contained more than enough adults, unlike prior villages she'd encountered.

She restrained a growl as she realized who the lich preyed on.

Striding back to Plodder, she began planning her attack.

"You dare to intrude."

She whirled, mace and sledge hammer in her hands.

The sound of a cloak billowing over snow made her tense.

"Come now. You should have better manners than this considering your age."

Z'ronia hated when a lich made a remark about her age.

As if they could sense how many years she'd lived whereas she couldn't tell theirs.

"I'm passing though," she countered calmly.

"Really?" The voice sneered, "Not with that spell, Grasper."

Other liches snarled the same insult so Z'ronia stood unaffected, waiting for the next move in their dance. The dance of final death to one of them, though she intended it to be the other lich's rather than hers.

"You are strange. Graspers always attack immediately."

Z'ronia snorted, using truth Grella unearthed to mislead, "That is not the truth and you should know it well. There have been all sorts and types of Graspers. From lawful to roguish, good to evil, and all those blended between. Not all with the same motivations and desires."

The lich chortled, "It fits with the delicious rumors I've heard of a Black Knight crushing his enemies to death and dealing vicious blows to detractors."

Vibrations began to rattle her feet, alerting her to approaching enemies.

"Just as I haven't heard of a lich who preys on the young and old," Z'ronia stated, "Clever you have been unknown until now."

"I have work keeping me out of the public view, in a way," a cloak slithered over snow, the rustling making Z'ronia move slightly, trying to act as if she watched the other lich, "Well paid for by higher authorities."

The whistle of arrows made Z'ronia dodge, lashing out with her weapons.

Knocking aside those she could, she felt the impacts of those she missed on her armor.

"I will enjoy making you my minion, Grasper."

Rushing steps made Z'ronia bark out the command with more power than she used with the necromancer, "Break your bonds and return to the other side!"

The clatter almost made her miss the spell, her mount's cry twisting her aside at the last second. Heat briefly warmed her side.

She went flying as an explosion struck her, tumbling her across the ground before she managed to come to a stop.

"I've never seen a Grasper move like that."

Z'ronia snapped out the next spell, using the other lich's voice as a directional.

Only for the lich to cancel out the spell.

Fear slowly curled in her, as Z'ronia weighed using the highest level of the spell Grella taught her. The one which took out all undead including the undead caster in an area, regardless of age.

Chanting began from the other lich.

Trying her next highest spell which didn't mean her own end, she bellowed it at the chanter.

The sound of ice slamming bone echoed into the distance.

No more chanting sounded, and she felt no movement.

"Air circle and thread," she murmured, "as if spun by the great Spider."

Her hearing sharpened until she could hear sound reverberating from all surfaces.

A chunk of ice sat where the other lich had been.

Moving carefully forward, she warily approached.

Only to jump as the Grasp of the other side rushed past her to burrow into the ice, leaving the ground entirely.

She heard a faint scream, before it faded away to the distance.

Kneeling, hoping she hadn't been led to a wrong conclusion, she dug through the snow to earth.

When she placed her palm on the ground and cast her spell this time, the clawing Grasp of the other side no longer waited.

This land returned to being like any other.

Shivering at how easily appeased the Grasp could be, she straightened.

Moving around to Plodder, she touched his forehead, "It's best for you to run if we find another one. You cannot aid me with those undead."

Plodder bumped her shoulder, the metal barding clinking on her armor.

"Let's keep going, preferably to the next village before we rest. I don't want to meet the higher authority mentioned," she mounted up, casted her directional spell.

Cursed.

"We are going west. We need north, my friend."

Plodder whinnied as if to counter what she stated, moving off.

"I am at your mercy then," she dismissed thoughts of the lich as they continued on their way.

Even though it had been a close thing with her almost using the final spell she would ever cast.

Sighing, she knew she wouldn't be spending all her time going the wrong direction, even if Grella found it amusing when Z'ronia ran across all sorts of odd creatures and enemies in her wanderings.

Her mind turned to the past.

Rathi looked out the arrow slit as dawn stole the endless nights from her.

The King of Winter spoke gently, "After all this time, you still begrudge the sun its return."

Rathi rubbed her neck, "I feel as if I get more done in a single day of night, than I do any other day of the year. I am not merely attending to enemies, I am caring for my people and their livelihoods. Clearing roads of snow and fallen rocks. Collecting water, wood and food so they don't need to venture far from their hearths. The sun steals that away until it is nothing but daylight."

The guards changed shifts at that moment, bringing the younger addition into the room as one of the elders retired for the morning.

The King of Winter asked, "The Queen?"

"She hasn't woken as yet, my king," Siolobha replied respectfully as she took up her post.

"Let her sleep as much as she needs," the King of Winter looked at Rathi, "Assuming our welcome has not been worn away."

Rathi scoffed, "You've been coming here for three hundred years. Obviously the welcome is well crafted for your continued presence, unlike the demonic mage I dealt with last night."

The young guard looked surprised.

Rathi gestured, "Come now. You wish to speak. Do so."

Siolobha glanced at the King of Winter, then once given a nod of agreement she asked, "Why would demonic mages trouble you?"

"They come to steal my people upon their deaths. Creatures such as my seneschal and others with mixed blood are desired for near invincible warriors, once they are made into obedient undead like skeletons or carcasses. Since my lands have more than its fair share of those types, they come weekly to rob the graves."

"You are keeping the vigils for them," Siolobha bowed her head.

Rathi nodded, considering the sun as it reached the peak for the day, then began the route towards night again, "During the days of full light, if a wagon cannot bear the dead here to my keep, there's a chance the corpses will be taken. To weaken the undead such corpses would make, my people have to dismember the bodies, burn each in different piles, then blend the ashes and bones with animals. It doesn't prevent them from being used, just makes it easier to destroy them."

"There is no command you can issue to return them to the other side?" Siolobha asked.

Rathi pondered the sidhe's face, surprised by the question, "The only one I could command would be a vampire of my own bloodline. Why would you think otherwise?"

Siolobha hesitated.

"There is another undead who ensures those dead return to the other side," the King of Winter spoke softly, "We are trying to locate them again. Unfortunately, they aren't easy to find since they blend in with humans, far too well for our mages."

Rathi smiled, "I wouldn't mind comparing notes on our methods. If there is a command or spell to keep my people from such terrible fate, I would move the sun to bring them to my side."

The King of Winter cocked his head, "Really? I would love to be a spectator to such a feat. Do send a messenger should you attempt it."

Rathi shook her head, "You think I wouldn't find a way?"

"I would wager it well worth the waiting to see it first hand. However, I believe your night has returned."

Looking back, Rathi grinned, "So it has."

She nodded her head to the King then rushed out, taking flock form as soon as the doors opened to the darkened skies.

Chapter 8

Northbound

"Power snaps from our cold breaths"

Z'ronia dismounted at the edge of the new village, joining a line slowly entering the gates.

Plodder tossed his head, rattling his barding before pawing the ground as they stepped forward at a snail's pace.

He'd led them westward for several days before looping back east. She'd need to ask which village she found herself at so she could assess her next actions.

Grella's long hours of describing maps and sometimes carving them in clay or rock gave Z'ronia a chance she'd know where she was and which villages she'd encounter.

Though maps this far north were vague at best.

"Long way to come for supplies, Knight," a voice broke her musings.

She asked, assuming the speaker was a gate guard, "What shops would you recommend for supplies?"

The person beside her shifted, making a creaking noise, much like an ill-worn chair sighing, "Got a smithy, but not up to the caliber of your armor and barding. Feed is best at the Kicking Donkey, and best travel rations can be found at the Halting Horse inn, along with a room and stable. Got a bard, but he's not the best."

"Bard?" She loved listening to bards whenever she managed to cross their paths.

Songs, instrumental pieces, gossip all were readily available if one knew how to ask. They were the best ones to discuss kingdom affairs with as they both were outsiders and travelers.

"Not worth listening to, Knight. What's your business here in Trader's Last Stand?"

She knew then she was in the Free Trade Zone which was the last of the neutral kingdoms before she had to traverse the monster-hunter ones to her desired destination.

Plodder must have taken the route to exit the lich's kingdom as fast as possible. Plodder's intelligence echoed again in his actions.

"Supplies, news and rest," she replied calmly, turning her head to the side, then warned, "no pick-pockets preferred."

A nervous giggle sounded as the short individual skipped backwards, "Such nice armor. Just wanted a feel."

"There are those who'd take such liberties as a threat or an invitation for foul deeds," Z'ronia stated before turning her attention back to the gate guard.

"Don't mind the little girls here. They will be going on pilgrimage soon and are a little too excited to find their husbands."

Grella once explained marriage, husbands and wives to her. How new families formed from such unions and a selection of ceremonies from various places.

A pity Grella would never know of this kingdom's practices. She'd love to spend time asking questions and making friends while she was at it.

The gate guard coughed, "Really be gracious of you to let her behavior be forgiven."

"While I hold no ill-will, others may not be so forgiving, especially a prospective husband."

The pick-pocket giggled again.

The gate guard sighed, then recited a long list of rules the village adhered to, and visitors were expected to respect.

Z'ronia committed them to memory.

"Do you agree to hold with our ways?"

"Is there a provision should someone attempt to harm me?" She inquired, suspicious self-defense was not mentioned.

"Well, that is only for the villagers and the guards."

"So the villagers may attack an outsider, but the outsider cannot defend themselves?" She wished she could glare at the guard.

"Well, see, we..."

"Are you really spouting that nonsense off again, Jorete?" A new voice teased, "My apologies for him. We do acknowledge self-defense, but practice ways to ease tensions, like offering a round of drinks, or to replace broken items."

The gate guard, Jorete, seemed chastised based on his huff, so she replied, "That sounds more reasonable. I will hold with your ways and solutions."

"May I escort you to your first destination?"

"Aren't you busy with your own work?" Z'ronia could tell the new guard wore similar cloth and armor to the gate guard based on the rasping they made as both moved. The behavior of Jorete meant this one was higher ranked.

"As captain, I go where I need to. Come on."

Z'ronia walked beside the Captain, listening to the villagers as they made way for them.

"So, supplies or inn?"

"Supplies," she replied easily.

If she got all her shopping done first, she could sit in the inn a while listening to the bard.

No bard was useless in her opinion.

The frivolous ones saw and heard more than their manners intended, and those quiet bards could be the chattiest ones, assuming they were plied with wine or food.

"What supplies do you need,...?"

"I'm called the Black Knight," she replied offhand, "Food, water, feed for my mount, and iron ingots."

"Iron ingots?"

Z'ronia wanted some on hand should she need to reforge her mace or sledge hammer.

Fighting the lich made her nervous about what else could be sent after her. With raw materials she could more easily forge her weapons anew, even in the midst of battle.

She covered her needs by saying, "Some villages trade iron easier than coins."

"You going back south then?"

She didn't reply.

"Just so you know, none of the villages north of us trade in iron. They trade in weapons and slaves."

Kill monsters and endorse slavery. That mix did not bode well.

"Then I will ask for a tour of your weapon smiths after the other stops," she stated calmly.

By the time she felt her armor begin to cool and the noises around her ebbed slightly, she collected enough supplies to get her to the kingdom she wanted.

At the inn, the Captain introduced her to the stable girl, which allowed Z'ronia to explain Plodder's needs and that his barding was to remain on, for magic reasons.

Both of her companions leaned back from Plodder, their clothing rasping harshly with the movement.

"Plodder, go with the stable girl," Z'ronia ordered, concerned with the wariness the Captain demonstrated with his posture and his hand whispering over leather as if he made to pull a weapon.

Plodder neighed then tromped by happily.

Z'ronia fished out one of the coins she'd received with her purchases, identifying by its distinctive raised dots and deep divots, held it out to the stable girl, "This should cover any feed and hay with spare coins after."

The stable girl held her breath for a long moment, then squeaked out, "I'm on it, sir."

Turning, Z'ronia moved towards the inn's entrance.

The Captain asked, "Are you one of those mages from Sla'der?"

"I come from further south than you can imagine," she stated as she reached out to hold the door which swung open with a creak and brush of a breeze. The wood felt smooth and well tended under her grip.

A group of grousing people stomped out, muttering about the pathetic bard.

Stepping inside once it was clear, she moved towards the smell of food and drink.

Only to stop as the glorious strains from a deep, resonating instrument rang through her armor and soul.

She knew this music and relished it above all others.

It had no vocals to it, only the large instrument blown by a master bard.

This bard performed it far better than those at the long deceased Court of Impolin.

Vorbe resisted the childish impulse to stop playing and tell randy poems instead. He knew his voice was too soft anymore to sing them as they deserved, but he didn't think he'd make enough to cover room and board.

"Sing you bard!" One of the locals threw a wooden mug at him, "This music is horrible."

Agreement ran in the room as others began to pick up items to throw.

Vorbe braced for the onslaught, squinting his eyes so he could try to cover his instrument from any missiles.

A dark voice stilled all motion, "The March of the Impolin on Solbo. I thought this song lost to time."

Vorbe looked at the doorway to the dining room, then fought his instinct to stop playing the bassoon.

He travelled enough to know the stories of a particular warrior, clad in black armor with thin blackish green embellishments. An undefeated mixture of blunt weapons and magic, bearing down on the field as the embodiment of the Grasp from the other side. A stoic statue until an insult was delivered to him and then the offender would be swiftly on their way to the other side. Those undead who tried to kill the Knight were ended with a word of complex magic or with a charge borne with unfathomable strength and agility.

Yet he also knew of a bard who'd met the Black Knight personally, and who told of other sides to the Black Knight.

Hathethan had spoken in low tones in the middle of a desert, his hands rubbing nervously, "The aura of the Black Knight is truth. He stands as a storm cloud, bristling with lightning and fury. However none of the stories tell of the interests nor exotic skills of the Black Knight. He came with Grella, the Blue Knight, to the Archives of Echos while I was there studying a rare translation of the archaic Cavern songs. I watched them. Grella pulled a book of spells down and began reading out loud. I was so fearful, I didn't really listen to her, since the Black Knight stood as a golem above Grella. I swear if I moved, a lightning bolt would send me to the other side. Except I saw the Black Knight wasn't simply a sentry standing guard," Hathethan leaned closer, "To the end of the stars in the sky, he was listening to Grella, closely. Grella stated something and the Black Knight corrected her."

"Corrected how?" Vorbe recalled asking.

LICH EARS

"He rumbled out, 'The phrase should be alight upon the Towers and ring the warning bells.' Then returned to silence. Grella nodded as if this happens often, continuing. The Black Knight spoke ten more times, on various sentences Grella spoke aloud. Grella stopped, called out. Then the master of the archive runs out with a blank parchment upon which Grella notes down the very corrections the Black Knight had spoken about. They discuss for a few hours, then the master gets this stunned look on her face. I waited until Grella and her imposing shadow left then asked the master of the archive what corrections Grella gave her to cause such a reaction. The translation of Hourl's notes have been sacrosanct for centuries, and none dared to counter the acknowledged version. The new translations provided revealed a spell in those notes none could have found without the corrections. The spell to call an angelic mage to face a demonic mage. It requires a master mage to cast, but we'd never have found it without the Black Knight."

Since Vorbe heard that, he'd sought out the odd and quirky tales of the Black Knight.

There was one which confirmed this Black Knight and the Black Knight Hathethan spoke of were one and the same.

The Impolin had been Vorbe's kingdom, once a long time ago. He'd been the one to create the March of the Impolin on Solbo in tribute to his most regal ruler, Queen Elorid. He'd taught it to his students before he'd been exiled through treachery.

Some time later, as the tale unfolded, the Black Knight arrived at Impolin, supposedly a year before the Court of Impolin was blasted from the world by an unknown power. The oddity of the story wasn't the Knight's presence, but his reaction to hearing the March of the Impolin on Solbo.

The Black Knight, invited as just a guest at the request of a respected Caravan Lord, stood in an alcove, partaking no food nor drink while the nobles partied.

Vorbe's most gifted student, accompanied by his own apprentice began playing the piece as the nobles discussed a trade agreement. Most paid the Knight no mind and didn't watch him as the song rang through the hall.

Except both bards had stumbled on the crescendo as the Black Knight strode towards them along the edge of the room, head turning as if seeking something.

Only to halt beside the bards and seem to still entirely. Even the pervasive cloud vanished and the bards felt as if the Black Knight devoted all his attention to them.

Then at the end of the song, the Black Knight, who'd thus not spoken one word, asked, "What is the song's name?"

"The March of Impolin on Solbo," his student shakily replied.

"The name of the instrument used for the song?"

"The bassoon, an instrument my master crafted for just this song."

Then the Black Knight walked away.

Only that Black Knight would know the song name since none had ever asked Vorbe for its title, not even when he played it at the Coliseum of Music.

Additionally, no other tale spoke of the Black Knight asking for the name of a song nor the instrument used to perform it.

A voice jolted him back to the present, "So what? It's a terrible song."

Vorbe felt as if the temperature in the room dropped.

The Black Knight moved, all deadly grace and menace, the dark aura expanding through the room like a blizzard wind.

The heckler cowered back as the Black Knight stopped beside him.

The Black Knight tilted his head, then nodded, "Come with me."

Vorbe continued playing, fighting a frown as the Black Knight moved to the center of the room.

"Come here," the Black Knight held out his hand.

Magic shivered the air before two chairs slid from an empty table into the empty dance circle.

The heckler scoffed, "Why should I?"

"Because you are missing the true sound of the song," then the Black Knight made a new odd tale, right before Vorbe.

The ever standing Knight, sat on one of the chairs.

Then the aura vanished.

The heckler snorted, "Stupid knight."

Captain Alrith walked over, frowning a long moment, then sat in the chair.

Vorbe jostled as Alrith's jaw dropped, eyes bugging out.

"Why does it sound like that?" Alrith gasped.

The Black Knight said nothing.

"Hey, Captain, what does it sound like?" The heckler challenged.

"Come listen," he stood, then pointed, "Quickly."

Vorbe continued as the heckler sighed, then trudged over.

To fall into the chair.

The heckler straightened in shock.

"The March of Impolin on Solbo uses both the bassoon and the room as instruments," the Black Knight explained, "It was designed to sound different as one travels around the room, socializing, though the best spot is the center of the room, as that is where the Queen would sit. It is never the same as each room and its occupants change the sound."

Vorbe smiled, his joy in hearing someone realizing the subtlety he'd crafted into the song growing. It had been a long time since anyone had caught on.

Not since he'd left his home kingdom.

There was a rush to the center as the inn patrons vied for the prime position.

Only Vorbe noticed the Knight slip away and move to another spot, leaning against the wall.

He finished the song, pulling his lips away from the reed.

Everyone clamored to get him a drink and a meal.

Then to his surprise, a gauntleted hand held out a stone token banded by brass metal.

His heart clenched in agony.

The token of appreciation was a custom only found in one stretch of land spanning ten kingdoms, though this particular token bore the sigils of the Court of Impolin.

He took the token, rasping, "I've not seen one of these in a long time."

"And most likely not again, Master Bard Vorbe."

The sad tone drew his gaze up, to the Black Knight's impenetrable visor.

"How?" He asked.

"Your student, Tarben, mastered only some of the bassoon's range. I can tell you are the one who crafted it since you use all of it skillfully."

He fought tears, clutching the token of his dead kingdom, knowing only this Knight figured out who he had been.

A slurred and nasty voice broke the jovial room.

"Another poser? Captain you should toss this fake Black Knight out."

Vorbe stared at the drunk son of the Lord of Trader's Last Stand, Moyner.

Everyone was glancing between the Black Knight and Moyner.

Vorbe felt the gathering magic around the Black Knight, as if the Grasp reached out to claim the dead.

One of the more monstrous tales he'd dismissed proved to be true as the Black Knight braced to fight.

All for the stupid oaf Moyner who should know better.

Vorbe began singing, his hoarse voice filling the silence easily.

"Black against Blue,

A shadow to hue,

Both edged in green,

Of Kingdom Yereen,
At one, do not sneer,
For he stands as fear,
To both lich and fool,
Silent spell his tool,
Bear knight no ill-will,
Or grind beneath mill"
Eyes shifted to him as all the villagers stepped back.

It was a well known song, even this far from the Kingdom of Yereen.

The superstition that followed it would dull the situation.

Per belief, if a bard sang that song and a fight ensued, there would be many dead for the next day's vigil, because the real Black Knight would appear and end all those destined for the other side.

Then the Black Knight's voice trailed his song, "May I offer a round of drinks and food?"

Vorbe stared at the Black Knight, confused.

Moyner scrunched his face, "Ihovet Vapor."

The very expensive drink that bankrupted many a lord to obtain a cask.

The Black Knight reached into a pouch, dug around a few seconds, the innocuous action at odds with the legend of the Black Knight, then pulled out several coins, "This should be enough to cover Ihovet Vapor for the room."

Vorbe's jaw cracked as he stared at the coins.

The proprietor of the inn snatched the coins, "Of course, sir. Would you like some as well?"

"I feel fatigued from my travels and purchases. Would a room be available?"

In minutes the Black Knight was gone, Moyner mollified by his large mug of Ihovet Vapor, Alrith chatting with the heckler about the notes they'd heard, and Vorbe feeling like he'd want to be up early to catch the Black Knight before he left.

For all tales of the Black Knight since he no longer travelled with the Blue Knight's company, he stayed only a night before heading onward to some distant task.

Chapter 9

Boundary

"Sending those ahead to the other side"

Z'ronia stepped down the stairs at the crowing of a rooster the next morning.

Glad to be up and ready to go so early, she knew she needed to head out again.

Descending to the entryway, she set about making her exit.

Knowing she'd have to cross into the split kingdom of Laeb next, she felt compelled to journey as far as she could today and put some distance between her and the town before anything else happened.

"Would you welcome a bard for a little bit?" The voice of Master Bard Vorbe made her turn.

"Are you not the bard of this inn?" She asked.

"I travel as the wind, always drifting onward. Best I go now, so that when I return, I'll be more anticipated and enjoyed."

"I am headed north to somewhere few dare to tread," she replied, turning back to the exit.

His steps followed her, "To Laeb?"

Z'ronia entered the stable, frowned as the jangle echoed oddly in the tight space, then called, "Plodder?"

The neigh directed her to the stall.

She patted Plodder's head, "Ready to head out, my friend?"

A snort answered her, then the noise of a hoof scrapping the floor once.

She lowered her hands to the door as a rustle above her sounded. "Stable girl?"

A loud yawn preceded creaks overhead, "Sir?"

"Would you water my mount before bringing him to the front?"

"Sure," a thump on the ground, then rapid footsteps swept past Z'ronia.

Moving out into the road, Z'ronia felt her armor begin to warm.

"I am headed north as well," Vorbe stated.

Turning her head, she asked, "Is it to follow someone you find interesting?"

Vorbe chuckled, "In part, but I know there are several villages north of here who'd welcome me, even if they don't get my songs, they want the gossip."

Plodder's trots made Z'ronia turn.

A head bump and a trumpeting cry.

"Do you have a mount, Master Bard Vorbe?"

"I do but I rather call her outside the walls. Using just bard or Vorbe is fine, Black Knight."

Laying a hand on Plodder's neck, she cast the spell to determine north, then began walking where the spell directed.

Vorbe paced her, leather creaking with his movement as his boots stepped lightly over the ground.

Last night she hadn't noticed his scent as the room was filled with overpowering odors. Lemon, orange, oiled leather, wood, wax, another oil mixed with sandalwood, soap and his own musk.

He didn't have the scent of approaching death, but some sense of hers said he neared the end of his life.

Grella said as a lich, she'd know things intuitively living beings wouldn't. Sensing the approaching Grasp from the other side was one.

However this knowledge made her sad.

The March of the Impolin on Solbo would be lost to time, only existing in her memory until that faded, or she met her end.

"If it's not an imposition, would you know what happened to Impolin?"

Z'ronia turned her head to her companion, then back to the front, "I visited after the devastation. The revenants belonged to a large scale spell, meant to harvest the spirits of those who died."

Vorbe halted, "Harvest?"

She paused, "Most likely a lich of some power. Impolin was acknowledged as the most successful of the warring kingdoms in the region. The Impolin spirits would be formidable enemies under the lich's control."

"All those songs and arts, lost just for war? How is it such cycles are in humans and undead?"

"Undead and living are sides of the same coin, so cycles are like the flip of the coin."

Vorbe started walking again, "No tale speaks of your philosophies."

"Most would not care to be near me as I'm a dark storm cloud ready to strike down any offenders," Z'ronia thought those stories manifestations of insecurities and fear of unknowns.

Grella's knights never feared Z'ronia.

They just assumed her aura of danger part of her mystery and didn't delve in.

Each had their own secrets and mysteries they never wanted revealed, so they kept their curiosities silent.

Grief washed over her again, making her grip Plodder more firmly than she intended.

"Since I will be traveling with you, are there songs you prefer?"

Z'ronia shrugged, "Songs of any type. Instrumental, vocal, a group, solo, they all are enjoyable to me."

"Sad, happy, angry?" He asked.

"All appeal," she frowned as she heard gate guards ahead performing checks.

She disliked exit checks of her bags and person. Yet another reason she avoided major places where they performed additional security on exiting a village rather than entering it. She preferred those performing the same checks going in as well as out. It felt more fair than doing it lopsided.

The spell she cycled up was one she detested.

Grella made her perfect it since she may have to remove her helm or armor to dispel suspicions on her true nature.

Only the spell made her very itchy, all the way inside her bones. Where she couldn't scratch to relieve the sensation. She'd have to let the side effects wane, though she hoped it wouldn't take weeks like the last time she used it.

"Open your bags," a guard ordered when they got to the front.

Flipping open the saddle bags, then setting her backpack down, she opened it up as well.

They rummaged through the bags, then demanded, "Helm off."

The spell took as she lifted her helm off easily.

Vorbe finished tying his bags closed again just as the gate guard ordered the Black Knight to remove his helm.

He shouldered his bags, using his side vision to watch the Black Knight.

The gate guard stammered, "I am just doing my job, sir."

The deep set, disapproving scowl on the knight's face only entrenched the glare in the black eyes. Fine wrinkles spread from the corner of the eyes as the short, blond hair waved in the breeze blowing by. Thin lips pursed as if holding back a rebuke on an opponent.

No wonder the guard looked worried.

If that look turned on him, Vorbe would run and hide.

The silence stretched, the eyes never shifting.

The gate guard gulped, "You can put your helm back on, sir."

As soon as the helm was on, Vorbe felt a shiver of magic in the air.

The cancellation of a spell.

Intrigued, Vorbe considered his companion as they were given leave to pass the gate.

The Black Knight set his items to rights then walked by.

Vorbe scurried in his wake, his curiosity piqued to the point he'd walk to the other side and back to know more about the Black Knight.

They walked in silence for an hour, putting distance between them and the gate guards.

Just as he was about to ask what spell the Black Knight cast, the Knight asked, "Your mount?"

Flustered, he pulled out a drum, embarrassed he forgot to summon his mount.

Curious how the Black Knight would react, he thumped the calling song, listening.

A bugle followed, high and eerie to those who didn't know what it belonged to.

Vorbe smiled as a glitter formed in the distance.

He stopped playing to watch the Black Knight.

Waited for him to react.

In any way.

So focused on the Knight he flinched as his mount nudged him.

Plodder neighed in greeting, the only reaction to his mount.

"You don't know what my mount is, do you?" Vorbe blew out a breath as he patted a nose before offering a carrot from one of his bags.

"A diamond doe," the Black Knight replied.

Vorbe wilted a little, "You've encountered them before?"

"I've heard the cry before, deep in the Mired Mines. My companions told me what made it."

Vorbe sighed, turning to his mount, "Sorry, my lady. No surprises today."

The light glittered through her frame as she pawed the ground, nibbling the carrot in obvious delight.

She wasn't a clear diamond doe, which was the most sought after. She was a chocolate diamond doe, which made her seem less ethereal than the clear ones.

After putting a blanket over her, he added his bags then strapped them down. He hefted himself up onto her back, then gripped the bags for balance.

The Black Knight stepped up onto Plodder, then set off.

"I usually get a few gasps, or oohs out of people when they first meet my mount," Vorbe grumped.

"If you truly wanted that, you would have brought her into Trader's Last Stand."

He pondered it a moment then laughed rustily, "That is true. However, I'd be fighting off every merchant wanting to purchase her. That's too much attention, even for a bard."

"Where did you two meet?"

"She'd been part of a herd the Orvin Lord kept. He'd been drinking heavily and wagered no one could best him in ocean cards. I'd been clearing out everyone else and came over to see who was issuing the challenge. I saw her then. He was using her as a chair, and really didn't pay mind to her health. Her light was murky and dim. I said I wanted to have one thing without argument should I win. He wanted my bassoon for the rest of my days should he best me."

The Black Knight tilted his head, "You won, since she's here."

"Technically, I did win, but he was a nasty drunk and magicked the ocean cards into dust before asking with this manure spewing grin, 'What game?' before laughing as he left the game room. Well, he'd broken his word so I felt no compunction to let him get away with it. I stole her while he was sleeping and made like the wind. I intended to take her to one of the caves her kind flourishes in, but every time we reached one, the herds would drive her out. So we ended up being partners."

"Does she or you have a preferred name she uses?"

"Octave. She answers to Octave," Vorbe rubbed her neck, "She's a great companion and gets me where I need to go safely."

"Due to some special spell or gift?"

Vorbe shrugged, "I don't know. When she's around nothing can harm me. She's like the ultimate luck. There have been times when I should have died, but the spell, attack or accident turned aside harmlessly."

The Black Knight fell silent.

Vorbe pulled his bassoon, did some tuning, then began playing a traveling song as Octave and Plodder carried them towards their destination.

If he placed his pile of coins correctly, the Black Knight headed to the kingdom of L'pilth. To reach it, you had to cross the Boundary, the land where the kingdoms south of L'pilth cleared so they could kill anyone trying to enter L'pilth.

Chapter 10

Warning Posts

"Under us Grasp claps with each victory"

Z'ronia found traveling with Vorbe to be both easier and more challenging.

The habits of traveling with living beings came back to her as if she rode with Grella and her knights again.

The illusion spell prevented any reaction from Vorbe when she lifted her visor or set the helm aside to eat and drink.

Contrary to belief, she could eat and drink without having it flow through as a mess.

Whatever magic animated liches enabled them to consume food and drink though there was no benefit to it besides enjoying the sensations.

Other habits returned like pausing for rest, answering nature's call and alternating between riding and walking.

Plodder found the later strange since she hadn't done it before while traveling with him, causing him to anxiously pace beside her.

However it worked well for Vorbe who needed such changes as they worked their way north.

He talked at length about the lands of Laeb and how they were traveling through Laeb East.

While Laeb could be considered one kingdom, it was divided into two major houses: House of Prince Nir and House of Princess Jirl.

House of Princess Jirl controlled Laeb East and ruled with slightly more compassion than House of Prince Nir did with Laeb West.

Princess Jirl wouldn't outright kill travelers who entered her lands, but if you broke one rule, off with an arm or leg.

Z'ronia didn't like this, since she wouldn't let anyone harm her or her companions.

The thought momentarily confused her, since she hadn't borne such sentiments since she parted ways with Grella.

On the other gauntlet, she hadn't travelled for long with any living person for decades. Maybe to the next village or even city, but never to another kingdom, much less across two. Only her mounts had that honor since Grella.

The challenge bit turned out to be when Vorbe's attention suddenly focused on her.

She may not be able to perceive his gaze, but he seemed intent on her after one of their evening meals. He didn't speak during these intense times nor move nearly as much.

As if he was hunting her like a wild beast and the least sound or scent would send her bolting.

She didn't like the sensation, nor the implications if that was his intent.

Plodder came to stop suddenly, then stepped back.

"It's the Boundary."

"Boundary?" She heard tales of a section of land no one should cross unless they had a death wish.

"We are a day's ride out, but the warnings begin here. The closer we approach, the worse the sensation."

Dismounting, she wanted to understand the spell.

Placing her hand on the ground, she sought out the warning.

Only she ran into an old elemental spell.

It wasn't the one causing the alarm as it was inactive.

Concentrating on the old spell, she tasted its purpose, smelling how long since it last was active, and touching it curiously.

Earth based.

It felt so old she wondered if it was older than her.

She rocked as she realized its purposes.

The first was to give warning when an enemy crossed, sending that warning to any elementalist who could hear it.

The spell stretched a great distance, at least the width of three kingdoms, possibly more as the far reaches faded out of her senses. Which enabled its second function: to allow an elementalist to move through the ground directly to where the warning sounded.

The last time it had warned was yesterday.

"This land has always belonged to Laeb?" She asked Vorbe urgently.

"No, L'pilth's once a long time ago. Before King Rathi's reign and possibly before, hmm, Queen Wralt's."

No elementalist had touched this spell in decades, possibly centuries.

Listening a moment, she weighed her options.

She could use the spell to move through the ground, explore its reach easily.

Carrying her mount would be a bit of a lift if she brought him along, but possible for a short jaunt. However it would leave Vorbe and Octave alone.

She didn't trust this land.

Pausing, she wondered why.

Pressing her hand deeper into the land she sent out another spell, seeking the answer.

She felt winter bound ground as it began to warm towards spring, roots slowly reviving as they prepared shoots for grass. A few burrowing creatures waiting for the moment to uncurl from their dens and begin foraging.

With a jolt, she knew then what was missing.

Even when there was no spirit to be taken, the Grasp always could be sensed on the outer reaches of her range. Like a wolf pacing nearly silent at the edge of camp.

Save now.

It wasn't even present.

Alarms shook through her as she realized she hadn't sensed it once since they entered Laeb.

Grella's words seemed to ring out over the land as if urging her to listen to the past, "This spell was supposedly used by the undead who associated with the Grasp from the other side. Servants to its will and whims. They could call on it to answer them when something prevents them from communicating some other way."

A minor spell but it may yield her a key to this strange and oppressive weight on her shoulders.

She whispered softly and with great respect, "To thee who all bend knee, what blocks thy will upon us all?"

Vorbe asked, "What was that spell?"

Before she could reply, a scream deafened her.

"Corruption. Run."

Z'ronia leapt unto Plodder, gripped Vorbe and lifted him unto Octave, "Bolt."

Plodder whined but jerked into a gallop, breath heaving.

"What is it?" Vorbe demanded.

"Lich," as she said it, she knew it was truth, "A very powerful one."

"There are no tales of liches this far north."

"Because its pretending to be the Grasp in this kingdom," she shivered as the spell she cast continued, racing beside them as it whispered the Grasp's will, "Stealing the spirits from the Grasp and blocking the Grasp entirely from this land."

"We will be exhausted long before we reach the next kingdom," Vorbe's voice quavered.

"We do not want the lich to find us. The spell I cast should be covered by my protections, but if this lich is far more powerful, then it will realize what has happened. All I can do is slow it down and clear the way for us."

"How? Liches are powerful beings."

Lifting her head she called out, "Thundering heavens scream your outrage upon this land, covering those honorable as they flee the enemy behind," adding the words to expand to the widest area she could power while leaving her some magic for smaller spells.

Vorbe inched Octave closer to Plodder, "There is no mortal born who can cast something a lich can't cancel out."

The elementalist spell beneath began drumming out.

"It's coming," Z'ronia cursed, willing the storm to form sooner.

"Liches have undead mounts. It will catch us simply because it never tires."

The drumming increased in tempo.

She hissed so Vorbe wouldn't hear, "Grasp, tell me what to do so you may claim me when my time comes."

As if the Grasp reached into her mind, it directed her to part of the incantation she used to analyze the old elemental spell.

It also guarded tunnels deep in the ground.

Tunnels which led towards the next kingdom.

"Follow me," Z'ronia ordered, turning Plodder towards the ground above one of the tunnels.

"You've never visited this land. There is nothing that way," Vorbe insisted.

She didn't argue instead focused her next spell, crafting it so it would leave no trace.

Thunder rumbled overhead as wind shrieked pass them, instantly dropping the temperature.

Rain came pelting down on them, clinking off her armor.

She snapped the word, activating her spell.

"Go down the slope Plodder," she ordered, reached out and tapped Octave, hearing the crystal ring from her metal finger, "Follow us."

Plodder plowed downward, heaving breaths as the clinks on her armor became more like clangs.

Then blissful silence as the ground above them sheltered them from the storm.

"Vorbe, Octave, keep moving forward. I have to seal the entrance."

Vorbe's pained rasp made her whirl to him, "I guess Octave's luck doesn't extend to storms."

She reached out and touched Vorbe, sending a spell she learned from a healer into him.

Wincing at the damage hail made on his body, she cursed.

"Give me a moment to seal the entrance, then I'll heal you."

"What spells don't you know?" he chuckled, then groaned, "Ow."

The spell to revert the ground back echoed in the tunnel before she began the incantation involving water magic.

Each healer's magic operated differently, but she'd learned from all she encountered by listening and feeling their magics while they reversed wounds, cured diseases and, in one case, resurrect a newly deceased back to life.

The resurrection demanded a life for a life though.

Chanting the almost song, she held out her hands over Vorbe, using a small bit of her magic to repair the damage and to warm his chilled skin and fragile lungs.

"How did you know about this tunnel?" Vorbe asked as her chanting echoed away into silence.

"I used magic to analyze an ancient sentinel spell over this land. The sentinel spell warns if enemies come over the land and through these tunnels. We were lucky one was near the surface," she touched Plodder, began a healing spell for her exhausted mount.

Then she touched Octave.

She'd never touched one before and found the warmth emanating from its crystal surface comforting.

The spell assessing her condition proved she had a small crack in her rear hoof.

Kneeling at the wounded hoof, she adjusted her healing to better serve Octave.

When she sat back, Vorbe whispered, "I heard once a diamond doe starts to crack, nothing could heal them."

"Octave is more of the earth than of the flesh. The spell needed to be closer to mend earth like the one I used on the entrance, than the one I used on you, Vorbe."

Vorbe could hardly see in the darkness of the tunnel now the healing magic faded from sight.

Octave gave off a faint light which let him know she was near, but Plodder and the Black Knight were shrouded from his vision.

"If this tunnel was long sealed, the air may be deadly to us," he pointed out, his voice echoing around him like restless spirits.

The Black Knight's voice filled the tunnel with a word in a strange language, then the air smelled better to Vorbe.

"This air pocket will follow us until we surface again."

"Would a light be available? I can only see Octave."

There was the sound of rummaging, then a soft red light brightened the tunnel.

The Black Knight tied it onto the saddle bag, letting the glowing rock bounce in what looked to be a tiny net.

He drew out a second one, made it light, then handed it to Vorbe, "These will need to be repowered, but will give a few hours of light."

Comforted by the little rock, Vorbe tied it to one of his bags, looking around.

"The tunnel looks to be carved rather than natural."

"I agree. The earth is trying to reclaim it, but it will be time before it collapses back to where it should be."

Vorbe looked at the Black Knight, "You conjured a storm, moved the ground then healed me with water droplets. You must be the most powerful elementalist in the world."

"Powerful, but I doubt I rank among the top mages," the Black Knight rubbed Plodder's nose, then opened a satchel to hold an apple for him to eat.

Vorbe leaned back against Octave, thinking.

Then his mind halted as he recalled what the Black Knight stated in their frantic dash for safety, "The spell I cast should be covered by my protections, but if this lich is far more powerful, then it will realize what has happened."

For a human, liches were always more powerful.

Yet he'd stated this as if some liches were not as powerful as him.

The odd need to cast spells when pulling off his helm, only to release them once the helm was back on led to a conclusion on the Black Knight's true form.

There were few things able to stand up to a lich or match them in sheer power: Angelic mage, demonic mage, or another lich.

It would explain the capabilities of his companion if he was an angelic mage, as well as the spell he cast before revealing his face.

Angelic mages wore their heritage in two features: their eyes were like a reflection of a clear night sky full of stars on a still lake, and their ears looked like the frills of some exotic fish.

Other bards said the number of frills covering the ears correlated to the age of the angelic mage, and possibly power level.

The spell must overlay the Black Knight's features so his ears and eyes could not be seen as abnormal.

Vorbe began crafting his version of the song for the Black Knight. It would have to be instrumental, which was a challenge.

A spelled song would ensure he conveyed the meanings regardless of listener.

He hadn't made such a song since his Queen requested one for the birth of her daughter.

The Black Knight tapped his mount, "Follow, Plodder. If you get tired, let me know."

He started forward, moving easily in the tunnel.

Plodder's hooves echoed as thunder down and back to them, distorting sound.

Vorbe walked behind Plodder, Octave following him.

The red light didn't reach far, but it alleviated the claustrophobic feeling of being deep underground.

However, as they travelled, Vorbe listened to the echos and the acoustic qualities.

With the right song, the tunnel could be an amazing hall for listeners.

"We will rest here. No fire," the Black Knight's voice jolted him from his contemplations.

Vorbe blinked at the alcove slightly lifted off the floor.

He felt all his years then, pressing down on him to lay down and sleep a century away.

Pulling off his bags from Octave, he patted her, "If you want to wander, just be careful, my lady."

Octave nudged him then trotted out of the light, fading into the distance.

Vorbe set up his bedroll, then pulled some jerky to gnaw on, even though his jaw ached from the effort.

"Do you think the lich will follow us down here?" He asked.

"The alarm has gone silent, yet the spell is all around us. Most likely the storm erased what little evidence left by my spell to get here. It is a known issue with large scale spells. Assassins love such times as their minor magics can be hidden or washed away before anyone can find them."

"There's a story behind your knowledge I am eager to hear," Vorbe stated, looking up at the Black Knight, the illusion spell up as the helm came off.

The Black Knight pulled out some hard crackers, began eating slowly, "Assassins love to try themselves on legends. I often cross paths with royals and others of power, so reviewing assassins mid attack is possible."

Vorbe snorted, "That doesn't make a good story."

The voice sounded with a slight smile, but none graced the Black Knight's lips, "Nor song?"

"Captured," Vorbe chortled, "Your songs and tales reach far and wide, but none contained any hint of assassins. It's usually some local who stands up to your tyrannical ways."

"Word of mouth changes all tales from their original form. The songs of Grella, the Blue Knight have all but obliterated the wonderful person she was."

Vorbe practically felt the grief frothing around the Black Knight.

"Are you willing to share stories of her? At least this way some part of her truly continues?"

The Black Knight seemed to look down the tunnel, back the way they came a long moment.

When Vorbe thought he'd get no answer, the Black Knight spoke with a soft voice, "Grella wanted to be a knight in a company since she was little. She joined every competition, every trial she found and won, each time stepping closer to knighthood. She was taken in as a squire under the Knight of Dusk. He was a harsh master but she persevered until she gained the right to enter the Sands of Honor.

"She fought and won on that battlefield like all other knights. Then she was told none of the companies wanted her. To lesser beings, they'd turn aside from such a formidable barrier. Grella instead set out to form her own company, one where she and others would be brothers and sisters in arms. She found me first, and taught me how to be a knight. Sol'gu, the Red Knight came next. He would drain a tavern of their ales and beer but in the fight, you wanted no other at your side or back with his grand halberd and giant's body. The Green Knight, Velia, was slight in height and girth, but she was fast, moving around enemies distracted by Sol'gu, Grella or myself. Many enemies never found out who brought them to the Grasp wasn't the brawny ones, but the small, overlooked one. The Yellow Knight Ophielen would talk even a group of bards into exhaustion, but none could overlook her skill in the crossbow."

Vorbe wondered why the Black Knight stated the colors of the knights with an odd tone, but he became engrossed with the image of the company riding into a town, the Blue Knight in the lead, followed by the Black Knight and Red Knight, then the brightly colored Yellow Knight, allowing the Green Knight to be overlooked or considered a squire. The stoic Black Knight needing no words as opposite the talkative Yellow Knight, then the minuscule Green Knight opposite the giant Red Knight who shook the land with each step.

"Grella led our company for over two decades, bringing us back to the King with more and more accomplishments. A vicious dire crocodile was no more challenging a task than helping find a lost child. Accolades mounted around us, but so did the jealous and vain who wanted us to fall," the Black Knight blew out a breath, eyes distant, "Sol'gu was poisoned with the beer he loved the same night Velia was hung from the warning tower, bereft of her armor. Then Ophielen fell to enemy magic while separated from Grella and I in the War of Borders."

Hatred burned the air even though the tone remained level and calm.

"Grella recruited others: Kirno the Purple Knight with a voice like rain on leaves, Shirth the White Knight with magic and knowledge,

Knot the Orange Knight whose spear pierced everything, even his own armor. In time only Grella and I remained. Then she sent me away."

"Why?" Vorbe suspected it was for the same reason the Black Knight looked to be reasonably young despite the years he'd served beside Grella.

"I do not age like others. Questions began circling as Grella aged while I remained unchanged," Bitterness filled the voice, "She asked I leave and travel outside the kingdom. To places where the Black Knight is a myth, a legend, a warning, a symbol. She aged as she continued as a Knight, but without a company even she had to give up fighting eventually. Grella settled in a village and taught the children how to fight and be knights. Many knights who roam now owe their acceptance to her efforts, both as the Blue Knight and simply Teacher Grella."

The Black Knight glared at the tunnel, "She died without friends nor family to hold her vigil. It was only luck I heard she had sickened a few months before and rode back to her with all speed."

"Did she make it to the other side?" Vorbe asked softly.

"She did," the finality of the statement sent shivers through Vorbe.

"Would you tell me more of Velia and Ophielen? Those knights are rarely spoken in songs and tales," Vorbe cautiously asked.

The Black Knight bit and chewed a cracker, then spoke with reverence of his long dead company, filling Vorbe's mind of knights long dead yet still rode beside the Black Knight on his lonely wanderings.

Chapter 11

Storm-borne Ills

"Those lived too long or not enough"

Rathi arrived at the village who'd sounded the alarm, her owl landing on the railing while the rest of her flock hovered.

"What is the matter?" She looked at the young guard standing at the bell.

She'd seen off the Winter Court across the Boundary a few weeks ago so she hadn't expected trouble so soon.

"The storm is wrong. Grappi says it's magic and powered by undeath," the guard pointed to the reclining elder wheezing shakily while others attended him, "He says the storm shouldn't be that large unless a lich conjured it."

Rathi looked out over the jagged spires which separated her land from the Boundary, then further out to the land of Laeb.

The storm grew unnaturally, clouds expanding in deepening bruise-colored and lightning crossed spans as if the air belched them out of a forge.

"It's been some time since a lich came so close," Rathi murmured, then to the guard, "Send word back to Darksteel Keep. Just in case they attack another part of the border."

Trusting the guard to do as ordered, Rathi flew towards the storm.

Arcing over the canyons made from the spires, she scanned for opponents.

Storms could hide constructs just as easily as living beings. It could be a full out assault, or a small band of enemies encroaching on her territory.

Daylight was still some time off, but it had grown in its reign over the land as spring came even to her kingdom.

Scouring below, Rathi watched the spiraling storm as lightning struck the Boundary with viciousness.

Someone had gone to a lot of trouble to conjure a storm more in keeping with the start of winter than the very end of the season.

Pain lashed her wings and backs, making her cry out as all of her flock plummeted, fire scorching her feathers.

Stretching her wings, she struggled to gather her flock into one as enemies descended from above.

Strange metal wings unfurled as the six humanoids slowed to a stop, pointing staves at her bodies.

Flame walls roared out at her.

Tucking her wings, she dove, fighting to get ahead of the fires snatching at her tails.

Cursing the other kingdoms, she wove through the spires, trying to avoid the heat, only to find it chasing her around corners and down into the gullies.

A flash of light preceded thunder by only a split second.

Then the rain poured in waves from the sky.

The heat on her tails vanished.

Gathering her flock into her body, she clutched the side of a spire, glaring back the way she had come.

The metal wings glittered as lightning struck the spires, almost like the bars of a cage.

One of her opponents twisted around a spire, only to be slammed by a bolt.

Shrieking metal striking rocks followed as the once living enemy fell smoking.

Five left.

Rathi hissed as pain in her side worsened. Touching the area, she felt warm fluid, just as she smelled her own blood.

Growling, she took flock form again, plummeting downward.

Normally her wounds healed immediately, but this time it didn't.

Flinging herself through openings she'd memorized over her centuries, she put as much distance between herself and those who'd wounded her.

She managed to cut through a sizable spire using a natural rivulet, before she ducked into a cavern at ground level.

With luck, they'd be forced to go over and chance a lightning strike or go around for an opening they could try.

Coalescing into her body, she leaned against the wall.

No burns lay on her skin, but a gaping hole spilled blood from her side.

She inhaled then pushed her fingers into the wound, seeking anything that may be repressing her healing.

Agony locked her body, closing her throat around the scream.

It seemed to go on for hours, days, keeping her upright but unable to move as the pain chained her as surely as iron or magic.

The pain even chased her into the blackness of unconsciousness, holding her prisoner as her life drained dangerously unto the rocky ground.

Z'ronia woke Vorbe before tending to Plodder.

The earth above greedily soaked in the rain her storm flung down, and they needed to start moving.

This part of the tunnel would soon flood with the excess the soil couldn't absorb.

The dripping echoing for some time began to flow in streams as Vorbe grumbled to wakefulness.

She stated, securing a strap on a saddlebag while she did so, "I suggest you call Octave."

Vorbe drummed out the song as he tried to collect his bedroll, failing to do either well.

In spite of the lackluster performance, the clip of Octave's crystalline hooves on stone grew closer.

Z'ronia stepped down from the alcove floor, splashing slightly as water seeped into her boots.

"I didn't intend this much," Z'ronia muttered as the streams noise grew in volume.

Splashing replaced crystal on rock.

"Can we get light again?" Vorbe yawned loudly enough to crack his jaw.

Z'ronia touched the rock she'd forgotten on Plodder, reigniting the spell with a whisper of her power, before reaching out for the one Vorbe had.

The weight of the rock in her gauntlet let her know he'd understood her unspoken request.

Reigniting the rock, she turned to Octave who snorted in distaste.

"Sorry, my lady," Vorbe shuffled, then swore as a splash sounded, "I don't like cold water either."

Z'ronia touched the wall as leather shifted over crystal, straps tightened slowly almost muffled under the cascade of water.

She felt the warning of the elemental spell, this time calling from the direction they were headed.

The lich must have begun a search pattern, maybe spiraling outward from where they lost Z'ronia and her company.

Jerking as she realized she hadn't dismissed the spell to hear the Grasp, she began to unravel it.

"One I do not wish, yet," the Grasp felt like it brushed through her armor to her soul jar nestled in the center of her ribcage, tingling sensations through her whole being, "Seek."

Confused, Z'ronia allowed the spell to lapse.

In the distance, rocks crashed against each other.

"Vorbe, mount now!" Z'ronia heard the rushing water strengthening.

She leapt into her saddle, turning Plodder to run away from the oncoming water.

Vorbe grumbled, splashing briefly before cloth rubbed on crystal, "I'm on, why do we need to go?"

"Bolt!" Z'ronia ordered, half turning in the saddle, whispering a spell to the tunnel behind.

The chill of being underground cooled further as she hoped the ice wall she formed would hold the water back long enough for them to get to an exit, or give her time to open a route upward.

"Plodder," she commanded.

Splashing, heaving breaths of two large animals, distorted echos as dripping or flowing water filled the tunnel.

"Black Knight, what is going on?"

"My storm is threatening to drown us," she heard ice scrapping behind them, moving as water swirled to touch her boots, even as she sat on Plodder.

"Can you stop it?"

Z'ronia cast out another ice wall, "I can only slow. Water finds a way through."

Octave squealed just before rocks sounded ahead of them.

Plodder shuddered as he tried to stop.

Only to slam into a firm surface, sending Z'ronia into it face first.

Shaking the ringing in her helm as the metal used her as bell clapper, she touched the surface, finding rock.

A spell confirmed the tunnel ahead had collapsed for some distance.

"The water is rising," Vorbe wheezed worriedly.

Plodder nickered uncertainly, shifted as water swished around Z'ronia's boots.

The elemental spell alerted the enemy was overhead.

"The enemy is above us. We will have to run or find shelter," Z'ronia turned Plodder, then cast the spell to open the tunnel upward, holding the end closed for now, "Up."

Octave didn't need further prompting, her hooves chiming on the rock as she raced upward.

Plodder slowly stumbled after.

"I'll heal you once we are at safety," she breathed to Plodder, "I may need my remaining magic to drive off the enemy."

Sealing the tunnel behind, they ascended the path.

This time it took longer, since the tunnel had dipped deeper than from where they started.

Z'ronia warned, "I'll have to open the tunnel to the storm soon. Tie yourself to Octave. I don't know how much more water lingers above us."

She could hear hemp rasping over cloth and leather.

Tapping the barding, she let the magic secure her to Plodder, freeing her to grab her weapons.

Too soon for her, they reached the end.

"I'm opening the tunnel. Brace," she yelled, adjusting the tunnel above, trying to carve out side tunnels for water to flow through based on her limited sense of the earth around her.

She startled as the earth parted exactly as she wanted, the whisper of it filling her mind as water raced by in the channels for the most part.

Rain soaked air filled each breath as they exited to the surface, drops striking her armor in waves. Thunder rolled around them, deafening her for long moments and making her uneasy.

Sealing the tunnel behind them, she listened to the elemental spell, setting the ease of doing refined earth carving to the side for the moment.

A new scent clung to her nose, blood with the taint of undeath.

"Vorbe, get behind me."

Octave clopped around behind Plodder as Vorbe had to nearly shout over the thunder, "Why?"

"Vampire," she pulled her sledge hammer, holding it in one hand, "Wounded based on the smell."

"We have to help him."

Z'ronia nearly twisted her head off her neck to make sure she heard him right, "Help him?"

"There is only one vampire in this kingdom, the King himself. The nearest ones are south of the country below Sla'der and Laeb West."

Cursing the bard for not explaining the lack of other vampires sooner to her, she nudged Plodder's side, "Move carefully, Plodder."

She hesitated to release the spell holding her to Plodder. With her armor nearly melded to the barding, she could focus on fighting with both hands, however if King Rathi was wounded, he may attack the first being with blood.

The alarm spell grew louder, indicating she closed on the enemies.

Then it gave her a total of them.

Five, hovering slightly above the ground around the next bend.

Pulling her mace, she listened through the thunder, cursing the storm she conjured.

Why did she have to make it so big? She may have gotten by with one half the power.

"It's daylight, right?" A voice bellowed.

"Yes. Let's go in after him. He'll be weak from his wounds."

The vampire blood scent clogged her nose, irritating Z'ronia.

Without reliable sound and scent, going based on feeling would be difficult, even if the alarm spell assisted her.

Leaning slightly forward, pressing lightly on his side then releasing, Plodder picked up her intent.

He trotted forward trumpeting a war cry.

"..at?" Thunder drowned out the first part of the cries.

Holding her weapons in a menacing manner Grella taught her decades ago, she roared a challenge, "Who dies first?"

Chapter 12

Spirit bound

"We will escort you to the other side"

Vorbe shivered under his cloak as he peeked around the rock outcropping.

The Black Knight sat on his mount, a dark outline against the grey rain.

Sheets obscured the enemy but for flashes of lightning on metal and the impression of human shapes.

They were either standing on a rocky ledge or perhaps floating.

"Identify yourself," a voice yelled back at the Black Knight, clear since no thunder rolled it to oblivion.

"If you don't know my name, then you'll find it out on the other side," Plodder stepped forward at some signal, snorting out mist just as lightning flashed, turning the breath pure white in color.

The rain eased slightly, allowing Vorbe to see the enemy.

Metal wings fluttered as five men floated above the ground with staves glowing with red flickering glyphs.

Fire staves. Fire could weaken an angelic mage if it was powerful enough. It was why demonic and angelic mages were both opposites and vulnerable to the other.

Overwhelming water like the storm could extinguish flames, but a burning forest could resist the rain and continue to reduce trees to ash.

Yet the Black Knight faced them as if unafraid of the staves.

One enemy flapped higher, "It can't be."

Three of the others glanced at the one who spoke while the last kept his eyes on the Black Knight.

"It's the Black Knight," the nervous one hissed, "The herald of death."

"The Blue Knight died ages ago. This is not the Black Knight," the one focusing on the Black Knight scoffed, before pointing the stave at the Black Knight.

Flames erupted from the tip, racing towards the Black Knight.

Only to halt halfway between the two groups.

Vorbe blinked, looking for the spell which held the fire immobile. He hadn't heard a word nor seen a gesture prior to the fire stopping.

"What made you think this paltry fire could do what Arlis' greatest inferno spell failed to do?" The Black Knight's voice slithered around him as if the words could touch him.

Vorbe stared at the Black Knight.

Arlis killed his king then dominated the kingdom of Irisan with his fire spells. Then one day a tornado ripped open his castle, razing it down to the dungeon. Those who spoke of it said a roar like a wildfire had preceded the tornado.

No one knew what exactly happened, but there had been speculation a lich killed Arlis, then made off with the powerful mage's body.

Without word nor gesture, the fire reversed back onto the stave that summoned it, then spread onto the man holding it.

His scream cut off just after it began.

A moment later, rain broke apart the blackened body, washing it away.

"Who dies next?"

Vorbe scrunched down behind his rocky cover, wondering if he'd survive this encounter.

When he'd mentioned King Rathi was the only vampire in L'pilth, the Black Knight's helm had whipped around so fast, he feared the knight suffered whiplash. Then an aura of death seemed to seep out of the armor, like some terrible beast beholden to the Grasp from the other side creeping into this side. He began to understand those stories telling of a monstrous Black Knight killing all in his path.

Swallowing, Vorbe watched the other four seem to side glance at each other, as if asking, who's going to answer.

Then the nervous one squeaked, shot upward with frantic wingbeats, screaming about the Black Knight.

The others chased after him until only the Black Knight remained.

He set his weapons back, then dismounted, moving towards a cave.

Vorbe walked closer, "Is King Rathi hale?"

"Unsure," the Black Knight walked into the cave as if nothing could harm him.

Cautious, even if Octave paced by his side, Vorbe eased to the entrance to the cave.

Blood spilled all over the ground, forming pools in places, growing tacky in others.

"A vampire shouldn't lose this much blood," Vorbe hissed.

The glow of healing magic made Vorbe squint at the side of the cave.

"Alive," the Black Knight seemed to draw inward, "Plodder, stand watch."

Plodder tossed his head, huffed before trotting around to face the canyon and spires, pawing the ground with his massive hoof.

The rain muffled the echoes of the pawing on the ground, but it made Vorbe uneasy.

Like the enemy could return and finish off the wounded king.

Stepping under the overhang so no water would fall on him, he moved to pull out his bassoon.

A scrambling sound made him leap back towards the outside.

Clang. Clang. Clang.

He whirled, to see the Black Knight holding King Rathi around his shoulders, an armored wrist jamming his mouth open.

Rathi's fangs gleamed as his feral eyes locked on Vorbe, his mouth opening slightly, then another clang ringing out as he chewed on the metal.

"Back up," the Black Knight wrestled the struggling king deeper into the mountain, "Make sure Octave is between you and him."

Vorbe shakily complied as the Black Knight muscled King Rathi back into the recesses of the cave.

If the Black Knight hadn't been so swift on his feet, Vorbe would have ended up dead at King Rathi's fangs.

Pulling his drum instead, Vorbe prepared one of his lesser spells for use with his second instrument, either to defend the cave entrance, or to flee the blood thirsty vampire king inside.

Z'ronia pulled the vampire back into the cave away from Vorbe.

She figured he'd go after Plodder first, being the closest blood source.

Lucky for Vorbe, she'd adjusted her reaction to ensure her armored wrist was between the king and his prey. She intended for her hand to cover his mouth, though.

"Easy," she rumbled to the vampire as she knelt, pulling the vampire down to the ground, "Give me a moment to heal you."

Her words went unheeded as cloth rubbed metal and the plip of blood or rain echoed in the cave.

Casting the spell to assess the exact undead nature of the vampire, she held on.

No other vampire was linked to King Rathi, which made the next part slightly more challenging. Grella once told her vampires and their sired children could be used to enhance spells against either the sire or the children by using the link as a guide post, both for healing and injuring.

She'd never healed a vampire before, yet she healed another undead: herself.

Tweaking the minor spell she used on occasion, she breathed the spell word.

The king clanged his teeth on her wrist twice more, then slumped.

Slowly easing away, her hand went to where she had discovered a wound on the king's side.

Now the flesh was whole.

Blowing out a breath she didn't need, she laid the king down.

"Vorbe, you'll want to keep clear for a while longer, just in case the king lashes out again."

Vorbe asked, "Healing undead beings with spells for living ones…"

Z'ronia sighed, "I used a spell designed for undead beings, though I had to tailor it to the king's type of undeath. It may not be exactly what he needs, but close."

Standing, she felt her vertebrae shift back into alignment, the tension in her spine and shoulders ebbing.

"What does the spell do?"

"Replenishes the source of unlife so healing is made easier," she tilted her head, "Vampires need darkness and I do not feel he should remain here with those four enemies knowing where he is."

"Vampires weaken in direct sunlight. He sometimes uses a carriage when the days are fully sunlight, so I know blocking sunlight works."

Z'ronia snorted, "You've played in his court long enough to know that?"

"I'm the only bard capable of crossing into his territory. Most others never make it out of the Boundary. He wastes a lot of time and energy getting caravans through so trade can continue and even then deaths occur."

She heard the affection and respect in Vorbe's voice.

Considering what she had on hand, she listened to the rain ebb away.

"The best I can offer is covering him in my bedroll and cloak," she moved towards Plodder, "Is there someplace close where he can find better shelter?"

"The best place is Darksteel Keep, his seat of power," Vorbe's answer made her want to sigh in exasperation.

Her first introduction to the king of L'pilth was to prevent him from gnawing on the only foreign bard his kingdom received.

"Get on Octave and ride for Darksteel Keep. See if they can bring the carriage while I defend the king."

"By yourself? I am not some old man with no way to attack nor defend."

She carried her bedroll and cloak over to the prone king, "You know the way to Darksteel Keep and, which ways only Octave can take, get there faster without Plodder and I slowing you down. The swifter the king is brought to safety the better his recovery," she turned to him, "Go now, Master Bard Vorbe!"

She flipped open her bedroll, laid it down before setting the King Rathi in the middle, wrapping him as best she could.

She wished she had Grella by her side once more.

When Grella gave an order, it was obeyed.

Z'ronia's commands were almost split in half on if it would be obeyed to the letter, or disregarded.

Much like her mounts, it was no shade of grey in the middle.

Vorbe's curse surprised her, "I will ride out for Darksteel, but I want you to use this. Tap it every minute and I'll know you are following. It will also direct you onto the path Plodder can manage."

With a jangle, he set something down beside her then raced out.

Reaching out, she picked up the item.

Magic course through her touch.

Musical instruments often acquired bits of magic from the bards who played them. Sometimes a favored spell, or simply a personality trait when played.

This one contained both, an indication of how long the instrument had been in Vorbe's keeping.

It had a directional spell on it, one akin to hers, so it wouldn't need sight to direct her. The personality trait was to play lively, something in opposition to her normal self.

"Plodder, come," she ordered, tying the instrument to her belt before continuing to cover up the king as best she could.

Plodder's heavy steps paused beside her as he nickered softly.

"Lay down. I can't carry him up then cover him with the cloak easily. If you can rise with both of us on you, that would be best. It's not perfect, but it should allow us to move out in the next few moments," Z'ronia finished with the bedroll, then wrapped the cloak over the king's shoulders and head, tucking the deep hood around his face.

Plodder thumped as he did as she asked.

Lifting the king, praying she covered him enough to ride out, she stepped over Plodder's back, sat.

"I'm ready," she said, gripping Plodder with her legs.

He managed to get to standing, with jerky and uncoordinated movements.

Yet they were up.

Linking the directional spell with Plodder, she said, "The instrument will guide the way. Follow it."

She tapped it, causing the instrument to jangle merrily.

Plodder shifted, then trotted out of the cave, headed in the direction the instrument indicated.

At least they were moving. Any enemy after the king would have to find them first.

Chapter 13

Crossed Paths

"Then march on to the next one who calls"

Ghir'ali rode the moose ahead of the others, scanning the cliffs and road for signs.

Of an enemy, of his king, or of a fight.

The bow laid across his legs as his eyes swept as far as the rain would let him see, his cloak forcing the rain aside, while limiting his field of vision.

A sound echoed against the cliffs, strange yet familiar.

He gestured to the side, halting his group and ordering them to make ready for a fight.

Focusing on the sound, he listened for its direction.

Having lived in L'pilth for his entire life, he knew how to read the cliffs in all weather.

Ahead of them, swiftly approaching, the echos told him.

He lifted his bow, notched his arrow and sighted, ready to loose death on the unfortunate noisy enemy.

Only for Master Bard Vorbe riding Octave at a gallop around the bend, looking as if demon mages chased him.

"Seneschal," Vorbe called, his hand on a drum, "The King needs aid!"

"Where?" Ghir'ali demanded, lowering his bow, but not un-notching it yet.

"The Black Knight is escorting him this way under makeshift cover. The king has lost a lot of blood," Vorbe pulled up next to Ghir'ali, "I can lead you back to them."

"Go," Ghir'ali lifted his closed hand and his group began riding out, "The enemy?"

"The Black Knight killed one, drove four others off. They were flying with wings of metal."

Kicking his mount into a gallop, Ghir'ali asked, "So a fake Black Knight is guarding our injured king? He'll be dead by the time we arrive."

"Not a fake," Vorbe insisted, "The real one who rode with the Blue Knight."

"An old knight is guarding the king?" Ghir'ali swore, making his nose decoration flutter violently, "Won't last long before the king seeks additional prey."

Vorbe rode ahead of them, leading down the paths back to the king, occasionally tapping out a beat on his drum.

Then the bard jerked, laying his whole hand on the drum for a long moment.

"The Black Knight has stopped tapping the instrument I gave him," Vorbe leaned over Octave, "Get us back to him, Octave."

Octave increased her pace, vanishing around the next bend before Ghir'ali could order them to stay.

Ghir'ali gestured to the group to follow while making the blood orb ready.

If the king was awake and feeding, it was best to have the blood orb ahead of them.

Six bends, a switchback, and through a tunnel later, he heard the shriek of stone on metal and howling wind, with catches of a drum sounding.

Gesturing to ride into combat, Ghir'ali drove his mount into the heart of combat.

Only for his mount to stumble to a stop as rocks shot into the air, leaving gaping maws where they had lain.

Beside him, a mangled mess of gore and metal slammed into the wall, slid messily to the ground.

Ghir'ali could hardly make sense of the scene before him.

A tornado of stone and wind lashed one way, then the next, spitting out gory lumps.

Water splashed upward against gravity, seeming to flood up along the cliff walls, before joining the rocky tornado.

It was something out of an olden story before Rathi's rule.

An elementalist standing alone against an ocean of enemies, calling out, "You will not prevail!"

Then earth, water, air, and fire joining into a massive army to bury the ill-fated enemy deep within the ground.

It was the last act of the elementalist, but it ensured this land was free for a long time before King Rathi came upon it.

Then the tornado eased, stones dropping from the sky.

He pulled back on his moose, trying to get clear.

Only to stare in shock as the stones slotted back into their places, fractured from the fight but otherwise once more in place.

Gravity asserted itself back over the water, pulling it back to the road to wash over the hooves of all the mounts.

In the center stood a war horse, its barding gleaming as lightning struck overhead, the black armored rider at ease while carrying a covered bundle vaguely shaped like a person.

Vorbe rode over to the Black Knight, Octave greeting the war horse with a nudge, the horse snuffling in return, "Black Knight, I brought the King's Seneschal."

The Black Knight nodded, "The sooner the king is secured in safety, the better for us all."

At an unseen gesture, the war horse stepped forward, the hooves splashing in the shallow stream the road had become.

Gesturing to bring the blood orb between them and the Black Knight, Ghir'ali tensed.

If this was a trap, it would spring here. If the King lashed out, this was the moment the blood orb would prove useful.

Nothing happened like Ghir'ali predicted.

The Black Knight passed the blood orb, only for the blood orb to follow the knight without a command from Ghir'ali's group, moving alongside to stay between the knight and Ghir'ali's company.

No, between Ghir'ali's company and the king, who hadn't moved inside the bundle.

Ghir'ali gestured to open the armored wagon.

With grunts, the underside was opened, the heavy doors held open by the other minotaurs against the spell attempting to reseal the wagon from the light.

The Black Knight stepped down, crouched, then lifted the body into the wagon, as if he'd done it thousands of times.

The blood orb slid by his shoulder into the inside.

Stepping back and clear, the Black Knight patted his mount's neck, the clinking of metal glove meeting barding clear in the air.

Ghir'ali stepped down, then ducked under the wagon.

He had to check and ensure his king was truly inside.

A reddish light gleamed inside, allowing a healer to see if they had to attend the king while in transit.

He uncovered the person, then relaxed as his king's face showed.

Gently pushing the blood orb closer to the king's face, he slid out.

A sweep of his hand and the doors were slowly closed, then latched shut.

"What injured our King?" He demanded.

"My assessment spells found no weapon. Only a gaping wound," the Black Knight offered.

"Spells for living beings..."

The Black Knight shook his head, "I used the spells for an undead."

Ghir'ali hissed, "You could have missed something."

"True. There are new and old spells which may have caused the wounds. Determining them would require a less volatile situation than this."

"Our mages will review," Ghir'ali stormed over to his moose, stepped up into the saddle.

A gesture sent the wagon and most of the company back to Darksteel Keep.

"Vorbe, you are welcome per prior orders. Your companion will have to follow our procedures for new-comers."

Vorbe turned, but the Black Knight spoke, "There's an alarm sounding."

Ghir'ali frowned, "Alarm?"

The metal gauntlet pointed, "That direction the elementalist spell is signaling another incursion."

Vorbe nodded, "You mentioned before you heard a sentinel spell sounding. Is it the same one?"

"Yes."

"You have to go," Vorbe held out a hand to Ghir'ali, stalling his denial, "Black Knight. When you are done, my spell will lead you to me."

"Be cautious. They may try for the king again," the Black Knight wheeled his mount around and rode away, the clopping hooves growing distant.

"Vorbe," Ghir'ali grumbled unhappily.

"I have travelled with the Black Knight for some time. He is as honorable as he is someone to be feared," Vorbe lowered his voice as he leaned closer, "He might be an angelic mage."

Ghir'ali ground out, "Or a demonic one."

"True. Please keep my words in mind as you deal with him. Treat him as you would someone both powerful and a potential ally."

"If he harms my king's people...," Ghir'ali threatened.

"I know my life is forfeit as is his. Shall we head to Darksteel Keep? I fancy a warm meal and dry lodging after this storm."

Making sure his mount paced Vorbe's, Ghir'ali glared where the Black Knight had vanished from sight, "I don't trust him."

"Trust is something earned. Just as I suspect those who know his true face must earn his trust."

Z'ronia rode through the canyons, discovering more and more surprises with each turn.

The land echoed with the spells some long ago elementalist laid to aid his or her endeavors.

Hidden paths, spells resting until called to arms.

Her tornado hadn't been intended to be of three elements, but the land joined in, almost gleefully, with earth and water.

The warning directed her through to the source.

Just as a clacking noise echoed.

Whispering so sound enhanced around her, she jolted at the clarity around her.

Cries of children, babies. Men and women shouting orders, replies.

Fire crackling.

Beating wings with odd wind against metal sounds.

Screams of the dying.

Almost too much cacophony for her to take in as she dismissed the spell.

She'd have to modify her spell to adjust to the land's aid, after she vanquished the foe.

More of the flying enemies based on the wingbeats.

"Plodder, defend the young," she ordered as they galloped forward.

The snort gave her his reply.

She leapt off, letting him thunder away.

Calling the air to give her voice more range, she yelled out, "Enemies of L'pilth, come meet your end!"

Only for her words to boom through the canyons, vibrating the air like thunder.

She needed to adjust all her spells involving the elements. Time was not her ally right now to begin the delicate tuning.

"Oh look, the king got a knight finally. Must be a young one," a light and cheerful voice taunted.

"What name should be stated at your vigil?" She demanded, lowering her voice to a threatening rumble.

"Oh look, it growls nicely. Must make the vampire quiver in excitement," the cheerful voice chuckled.

Z'ronia figured she would fight someone who either didn't know she was the Black Knight, or suspected but thought her reputation unearned.

Invoking the spell to ground the flyers, she winced as six metal thuds slammed the ground, followed by high pitched shrieks of pain.

Grateful for the full helm covering her skull, she moved on the enemies, drawing her maces.

"The Black Knight!", "He's here?", "The Black Knight knocked them from the sky" and "Put out the fires, quickly," sounded from the direction Plodder clopped.

"The Grasp will claim you," she stated, standing above one of the broken bodies, her boot clinking on the metal wing.

"You are nothing. Our master has struck the death blow to the king," the once cheerful voice rasped in agony, "This land will be his."

"Then I will guard this land until someone better defeats me," Z'ronia knew she could keep the promise far better than most mortals.

"I see you," a voice overlaid the rasp, "You are my prey."

The Grasp scratched under the earth, sending vibrations through her boots and up her legs. As if to say it wanted to collect the speaker, but couldn't.

She countered, "All succumb to the Grasp, even you."

Her mace made short work of the enemy, leaving corpses in her wake.

She whispered to the fire she heard crackling nearby, asking it to pull back into embers.

Walking pass a wall, she heard Plodder's neigh.

The cries for water eased as she walked into the village.

"Black Knight?"

She turned her head, "Who asks?"

"I am the head of this village, Lin. Those flying men claimed our king was slain."

"When your king left with his Seneschal, he was alive, but wounded. What do you need?"

"Need?"

"Healing, repairs, protection?"

"Those all are needed," the village head replied uneasily.

"I will start on the wounded. Are all of them over there?" She nodded towards where she heard those rasping or screaming out in pain.

"Yes."

She marched towards the noises, then got to work.

Time meant little to her as she cast her spells, gathering help from the land as it recognized her style of healing magic, forming droplets to ease the burden on her weary body. Cries slowly petered off to groans, then even breathing.

Standing once her area spell to identify the next wounded responded with none, she moved to Plodder.

Plodder bumped her shoulder, making a soft clang.

"You did well, Plodder," she softly spoke to him, "Keep guard until I've done enough."

A snort blew his breath into her helm.

She opened a saddle bag, pulled a carrot, then held it out for him to nibble on.

"Black Knight?" The village head's voice sounded as he'd just wakened.

Turning to him, she waited.

"You offered repairs?" He asked hesitantly.

She nodded, "Is everyone clear of the damaged areas?"

"They all are in the great hall. It's buried into the cliff face so it wasn't harmed when we were attacked."

"Good," she stepped into a clear space, gathering her magic and words into the action she wanted.

The original spell required her to know the look of the buildings. It took painful repetition and practice to make a version she could use without the visual component.

Blowing out a breath she called to the earth, the air, the water and even to the fire to reform the area to an earlier time.

To before the storm she summoned.

Yet she added something new as the stones and wood rolled and flew to their original places.

They would return stronger than before.

The stone would hold up against a giant's club, as wood doors would resist breaking from battering rams. Fire would only burn in places where it was encouraged by the village people, in fire pits and hearths.

When she shook her shoulders out, the echoes from around her sounded different. It must be how the village sounded before the attack.

"You returned the village to its glory."

"I brought it back to before the storm with some improvements," she listed them, feeling weary, "Will this suffice?"

"More than I hoped for. Thank you, Black Knight."

"I need to travel onward. Go inside the hall and I'll reinforce the door to match the rest of the village."

She cast the spell to make the hall doors stronger, then went to the dead.

She didn't often use this spell as it marked her as other. Near the dead, she chanted for the Grasp to claim them without a vigil.

It brushed her, stealing a bit of her remaining magic to do its work, shifting from one corpse to another.

Then it dove deep into the ground, taking the spirits with it. Any undead raised from these corpses would disintegrate in hours.

She saddled up, directing Plodder to go towards Vorbe.

She whispered a spell to tap the instrument so she could rest.

Her mind drifted as Plodder's motion lulled her into the closest she came to sleep.

Chapter 14

Revelations

"Until all have crossed over to begin the cycle anew"
Ghir'ali stood outside the room Rathi lay unmoving in.

The healers worked in the fire-lit room, ensuring the blood orb hovered over the king as they worked.

Master Healer Hagh and his best pupil, Healer Froda, worked spells, attempting to figure out why the king neither woke, nor fed on the blood orb.

The four Minotaur guards inside stood at attention, ready to pull the healers to safety and be food for the king should he bypass the orb.

Ghir'ali disliked he had to stand at the door, but he respected his king's wishes. If the king went berserk, Ghir'ali was to lock his room and prevent him from escaping. The whole kingdom would suffer if Rathi left Darksteel in search of prey.

Vorbe sat on the floor, softly playing on his instrument, a soothing noise against an otherwise quiet and tense situation.

Ghir'ali demanded, "Where did you encounter this black knight?"

Vorbe finished the chord, then rested his instrument, "In Trader's Last Stand at the Halting Horse inn, which lets me play but really doesn't understand my music. At least until the Black Knight pointed out how it should be heard."

Ghir'ali scowled, "Explain further."

Vorbe rubbed his scalp, the thinning hair swaying with the motion, "I was playing, thinking I wouldn't make any coin, possibly get smacked for my trouble, when he appeared. He knew the name of the song, said it out loud."

"Which song?"

Vorbe smiled sadly, "The March of the Impolin on Solbo."

"The one which echoes all the way to the kitchens," Ghir'ali favored it over most of Vorbe's other originals, and all he collected from other bards.

"It does?" Vorbe smiled, then sighed, "The Black Knight walked over to one of the hecklers then beckoned him over to the center of the room, calling two chairs with magic to the spot. The heckler didn't want to go, but the captain of the guards humored the Black Knight. He heard the song as it was intended and then everyone wanted to listen to it. He gave me a token of appreciation."

Ghir'ali frowned, "Like those cloth squares the ladies give the king?"

Vorbe chortled, "No. Back in Impolin if you enjoy a performance or art piece, you give the performer or the artist a token of appreciation. It is...was common for performers to have competitions to see who gathered the most tokens for a performance. I won a few competitions, lost others, but never did I fail to get a single token for my art. To have the Black Knight present me with such a token felt like both an honor and a blow. To be clear, I doubt the Black Knight meant harm."

Vorbe pulled out a stone wrapped on the edges with brass metal and etched with sigils Ghir'ali did not recognize. It looked as if it was fairly new, bearing only a few scratches.

"This has to be several decades old, but looks as if it was newly made. The Black Knight treated this as the honor it should be, not like most who visited Impolin and her fellow kingdoms," Vorbe rubbed the edge, "I received many tokens from ill-informed visitors which they wore down to nearly unrecognizable, missing the metal band, or cracked. To receive such from a fellow Impolin is a grave insult, meaning they think your performance was barely worth recognition. A back-handed slap if you will," Vorbe secured the token into a pouch, "I know he is the real Black Knight."

Ghir'ali fought the sneer forming on his face, "The real Black Knight wouldn't have the power to form those spells. He's too young and powerful to be the real one."

"It is said those of certain heritages live several centuries, and the older they get, the more powerful," Vorbe countered, "It would explain some of the stories I've heard in my travels."

Ghir'ali's snort flipped his nose feathers upright, "It's a young pup pretending to be the original."

Vorbe sighed, "I passed through Yereen a few decades ago. There is a difference in how the generations communicate. Most elders turn or tilt their heads towards who is speaking, some even turning their whole bodies. It's a sign of respect and honor from them. The younger generations intentionally turn their head away from the speaker, pretending they are disinterested. The Black Knight always tilts his head towards those who are speaking, often turning his whole body to face them. He faces them in a non-threatening manner. He's not acting like he's about to be attacked. He's behaving like the older generation who showed they listened by facing the speaker."

Ghir'ali grumbled, "Not every youngling will follow their peers."

"When their new king took power, all the younger ones followed his disdainful way of communicating. Bad blood between him and his father resulted in their whole culture shifting based on the son's popularity. The elders were bemused by the shift rather than alarmed. They play games where they mirror the actions of the younger generation. It's like a game of opposites. The younger has to decide to switch customs or continue like their elders."

Ghir'ali sighed, "You went down a side alley."

"The vagaries of aging," Vorbe sighed, leaning back, "If you only listen to the common songs, you miss subtle cues as to who and what you deal with. It has kept me safe these decades, knowing the exotic or nearly forgotten songs. I have met posers for many heroes and villains and I've been honored to met the originals. When you meet an original, there's an aura of magic around them."

Ghir'ali scowled, "What aura?"

"When songs are sung or art is crafted, those creations gain power, but so does those people who are featured in the song or art. It's why songs for villains mention them in a vague sense. To weaken what power they gain, but they gain the aura. The Black Knight has one of the most powerful auras I've seen save for a distant glimpse of an angelic mage. That angelic mage could be no other than the head of the Tower of Floods: Rhinopias Delaro. She has lived for three centuries and is a demonic mage's worse enemy. The bards tell of the rain lances she commands to fell her enemies even for battles before our mother's mothers were born."

"Surely imposters would have the aura."

"It is an oddity with magic born of the arts. Those pretending to be the originals, do not gain the power the arts imbue," Vorbe smiled sadly, "I have been fooled by imposters until my song proved they weren't who they claimed to be."

"Ghir'ali?" Master Healer Hagh called.

Ghir'ali stepped into the room, moved swiftly to the healer's side.

"The spells show no wound remains from whatever injured our king, but there is still a wound left."

"How can that be?"

"We must be dealing with a new weapon. We need to know what wound our king took, since Vorbe mentioned his companion healed our king. We need the information immediately."

Vorbe added, surprising Ghir'ali as he joined them at the king's bed, "The Black Knight is returning. I'll get him."

Ghir'ali snarled, "We will get him."

His hooves snapped on the stones with his fury.

The Black Knight should have shared everything before taking off.

A noise startled Z'ronia.

Soft, beautiful and asking for her to listen closer.

Lifting her head, she turned her head.

Wind brushed her, curling inside her armor as if hugging her.

Water burbled happily over the thunder of a massive waterfall.

Warm and thriving soil filled her nose with the burst of life spring heralded.

Even a distant crackle of fires called welcome to her.

Sending out a small incantation to determine local spells, she gasped at what returned.

Before her dominated the land with its spells, all intwined and connected to distant parts of the kingdom.

This had been the elementalist's home, and after such a long time of disrepair, the home recognized a kindred spirit.

It reminded her of Grella laughing as she pulled Z'ronia into a library or to the campfire.

Come join in. Be one with us.

She had no tears, but the grief welled as the land practically tugged her closer, offering a place to rest and recover.

Vorbe's spell led to the elementalist's stronghold.

Dwarfed by the magnitude of what that elementalist accomplished, she felt honored their home wanted her to enter.

"...Knight!"

She turned her head back forward, hearing Vorbe's voice.

Octave's hooves chimed over the noises as the wind parted around the diamond doe's body with a soft whistle.

"Vorbe, is something the matter?"

Why wasn't he at the Darksteel Keep? Had an attack struck?

"The healers need to speak with you. The king hasn't woken and they are worried."

"Lead," she commanded, "Plodder."

She didn't need to tell Plodder anything more as he thundered after the chimes from Octave.

She tried to recall all Grella told her of vampires, but she was drawing an empty bag on anything that would hold a vampire to sleep.

Had she missed something?

It began gnawing at her. Her failures usually resulted in massacres.

They came to the front of what sounded like a sheer face of a cliff.

Except the spells were brushing over her, letting her know it wasn't just a cliff.

Dismounting, she ordered Plodder, "Go with their stablehands."

Vorbe's creaking leather let her follow him.

The distrustful rumble of the Seneschal revealed his presence, "What wound did the king take?"

Halting, Z'ronia relayed, "A deep gouge in his side. No physical weapon was in the wound, though. My spells found no foreign elements inside."

"Come speak with the healers. If you make a wrong move, we have a sizable and varied dungeon for your new home."

She didn't doubt it.

Following the clops of the Seneschal inside, she tried to pay mind to the path.

New places sometimes screwed with her sense of direction so having both a mental map and her spells, she could return to the entrance if they decided to drive her away.

She rather not spend time in a dungeon when the enemies of the king could be taking advantage of this vulnerability to launch armies.

The Seneschal barked, "The alleged black knight."

If the situation had been less dire, she may have snorted in amusement.

The Seneschal was one of those who assumed she was a fake, if the tone proved true to action.

A softer voice drew her into the room, "Master Healer Hagh, Black Knight."

"What information do you seek?" She replied, moving into the room.

A sizable bedroom, based on the echoes and noises.

"What can you tell me of the wound you healed?" High inquired.

"A gouge deep into his flesh. It was barely bleeding by the time I started my assessment spells."

"Which spells?"

"Algrwe's Full Body Assess and Swerain's Probing Depth," Z'ronia replied calmly.

"I used both as well. Did you remove anything from his wound?"

"No. There was nothing foreign when my spells returned their results."

"The healing spell you used. What was it?"

Glad for her helm hiding her flinch since the spell could reveal what she was, she complied, "Renewal of Bone, modified for a blood drinking undead with the following words changed," she listed them.

"That is very close to the spell we use for the king," Hagh shared the incantation, much to Z'ronia's delight, "He should have waken."

"By process of elimination, then there is a weapon remaining or possibly a spell lingering," Z'ronia riffled through her memories for spells.

"You have a thought?" Hagh asked.

She found it, "At the library of Jorenette there is a copy of a very old assessment spell, replaced by the precursor to Algrwe's Full Body Assess: Ouwls' View."

Hagh wheezed, "That is practically a legend. It was expensive in power to cast, but needs no reagents."

Z'ronia assessed her recovery, how much magic remained, knew she had to chance it since whatever ailed the king could only worsen, "I possess enough power to cast it and the sub-spell to share the knowledge."

A long time ago she ran out all her magic. She collapsed and only Grella coming to her defense had prevented her being sent to the other side by marauders.

Since then, she didn't dare get close to the edge as she lacked allies. She stepped closer with this spell.

"Please," Hagh replied, pulling her out of the past.

She stepped around Hagh, then held her gauntlet over the bed.

"Place your hand on my shoulder. It makes the sharing easier," Z'ronia ordered.

She felt when he complied.

Incanting the spell took time, precision and patience.

To her time had really no meaning since she rode away from Grella. However to mortals, they felt it keenly.

Hagh shifted, his robes rustling and whispering against his skin, the stone floor and itself.

Vorbe's leather creaked as he moved about the room, changing places fairly often.

The Seneschal's heavy breaths permeated the room with his growing impatience and strength to back up threats he could make.

None of this distracted her from her spellwork, merely marking the passage of time.

She shuddered as the spell flared to life.

Fighting exhaustion, she focused on the magic as it did its work.

Almost as if someone had guided her hand over the most minuscule vein, spur of bone or toned muscle, she marveled at the details.

The king's strength seemed to be a match of her own as she felt the quiver of the muscles and their potential.

Very little blood in the veins meant the king should be feasting on the thrumming orb scenting the air with fresh blood.

Yet he lay still.

Z'ronia considered the next bit of information to flow through her. The king's true gender.

Perhaps they could be kindred spirits as they both walked the world as men, when in truth they were women.

Hagh tensed as the information flowed to him about the king's gender.

Not like he was shocked by it.

More akin to him being baffled why Z'ronia wasn't.

Happy her thoughts were not part of the sharing, Z'ronia continued to review whispers and touches the spell brought to her.

The flesh where the wound had been was smooth and undamaged, just as her spell intended.

She could feel and taste her spell's traces through Ouwls' View. That was different than the other assessment spells she'd cast before. They never uncovered the remains of spells cast.

She leaned slightly forward as the next traces turned out to be more from an active spell.

"That must be it," Hagh hissed.

Necromantic in nature, the spell also bore concealing elements, meant to blind both Algrwe's Full Body Assess and Swerain's Probing Depth from seeing it.

It drained the king of strength, forced agony, and held her almost immobile.

"I'll let the spell finish, in case there are more," Z'ronia began reviewing her spells for a counter.

Ouwls' View revealed no other new information but the king's age: six hundred and one years old, including her time before becoming a vampire.

Hagh huffed a breath, "Centennials are supposed to be celebrated."

The Seneschal stomped closer, "What?"

Hagh gave an exasperated sigh, "Our king is six hundred and one years old. We didn't celebrate his six-hundredth year on this side."

The spell ended.

Z'ronia breathed as she grew more despondent.

There was no spell she'd learned which could counter the one destroying the king.

Making new spells was dangerous, and for good reason.

The elements and powers out there could easily change from something meant to help, to cause harm to either the caster or nearby allies. Every spell balanced delicately on the tip of a pin so it did as intended and no more.

Many mages died or lived with permanent injures to make spells all others used.

Spell crafters were marked by their art in many ways.

"Master Healer Hagh, do you have a spell which could counter the one we found?" Z'ronia asked, hopeful he did.

"Nothing I've learned could attempt to touch such a spell. A lich's spell is practically uncounterable."

Embarrassed she overlooked the caster's nature, she tapped her chest, a habit Grella encouraged to be more human, looking over her esoteric collection of spells.

Grella's efforts meant she could use them as needed without incurring the penalties of crafting new ones. When Z'ronia made her own, she had time to make it as balanced as possible, softly letting earth, fire, wind and water to guide her to safer invocations.

Time was the enemy here.

Cobbling together a rough outline, she turned to Hagh, "There are pieces we can try. Would you be willing to review?"

"Pieces?" The Seneschal sounded close to murder.

"The Black Knight's proposal is the only remaining option to saving the king's life, Ghir'ali," Hagh snapped back, "We do not have time to make this spell perfect. Froda, join us."

Vorbe spoke, "I will offer what little I've found in my travels."

Grateful for Vorbe's tranquility, she prepared to share all the words she could.

"I'm calling our mages," the Seneschal stated before storming from the room.

"Let's wait for those here in the keep," a sound of skin over hair hissed softly, "Let's rest a moment before we continue."

Z'ronia didn't rest, instead working through her spell bits so when they collaborated, she could offer more.

Chapter 15

Discoveries

"Even those who made bargains foul"

The chamber howled with voices as four leaders argued, while the fifth sat waiting for them to find an impasse.

Alemific considered the demonic mages arguing over who possessed fault for the failed assassination attempt.

As one of the leaders of the kingdoms bracketing the kingdom of L'pilth, he knew patience.

The hateful elementalist four centuries ago may have blown his armies to smithereens, but he knew how to rebuild. To learn and conquer.

Even as the final words of that long ago elementalist circled his mind yet again from his previous attempt to conquer.

His armies spread around him as they trudged across the plain towards the easiest route into the land which would become L'pilth.

A towering wall broken in the middle by a river-etched canyon.

A frail and old body stood on the cliff edge above what hadn't formed yet into Lake Death, wind lashing the worn and fraying leather bits making up a cloak.

With a voice booming with age and vigor, the elementalist spoke with utmost calm, "You seek to claim that which does not belong to you."

Alemific challenged the figure with his own thunderous words, "With my might and magic, these lands are mine. You have no power to keep me from my spoils."

The figure snorted derisively, "Those with loyal hearts and brave minds will always face your schemes with victory. This land will be free of you long past when the sun scorches the seas away. Today, I am your enemy and bane."

Alemific cast a fireball at the elementalist, bringing his full power into it.

Nothing but ashes would remain of the old fool.

Only the fireball dissipated against lashing rain, snuffed out by an impossibly strong spell.

"I curse you to be defeated by this land, forever," the elementalist seemed to grow taller as the ground began shaking, lightning crackling like a thousand trees sinking their roots deep into the ground at the same time, a roar of wind circling into seven raging tornados.

Oddly the river halted its burble, going dry almost instantly.

"I give you the chance to leave with only half your forces removed from your will," the elementalist gestured across the wide ranks, seeming to smile.

Alemific kicked his mount, a carcass of a war horse into motion, calling down the arcane magics bound to his will. His armies began running towards the canyon at his mental command.

From his palm, arrows of light sliced out at the tornados, rending them asunder before tearing into the figure perched on the cliff.

It seemed all noise halted when the elementalist stumbled.

Only for the dreadful enemy to straighten as if renewed with the vitality of youth.

Alemific swore the eyes bore into him, laying a curse even as the words the figure uttered did.

"You will not prevail!"

The last word grew into rumbles.

The elementalist dropped out of sight, just as water gushed out of the canyon, crashing as a wave upon the ocean, when no such waters existed there.

Lightning struck, clipping his strongest undead warriors from the army with the precision of an archer. The seven tornados reformed, doubled in strength before charging into his armies, flinging his minions about like a child throwing a temper tantrum.

Frantically he called up his strongest wards, placing them to shelter his forces.

Only for the ground to split, tearing the wards and siphoning his magic away.

Then the waves crashed over him.

He tumbled, seeing flashes as lightning briefly illuminated the water.

Pulling in close, he warded his body so nothing would injure him.

It felt like days before the waters calmed, allowing him to kick to the surface, following his directional spell upward.

Breaking the surface, he looked around.

Pieces of his supply wagons floated all about.

Summoning them together, he raged.

The links to his warriors cut with the final destruction of their mortal remains.

Climbing on board the makeshift raft, he considered the cliffs.

He laughed, "I can conquer your land."

Smiling, he lifted the raft and himself into the air, hovering above the waters.

He had no warning.

Something shattered his raft, flinging him away from his new kingdom.

He didn't feel the pain until he sunk back into the water, the cold of the water cracking his bones as it fought the fire burning him.

Struggling with his weakened and almost magic-less body, he surfaced, clung to a barrel.

Too weak to attempt flying again, he looked back towards the cliffs. Only to find one of his eyes was blinded.

The other filled with the red plumes of molten lava erupting in multiple places, creating spires as well as sealing the canyon way.

Where he'd been flying, a growing mound of lava sputtered into the sky, throwing heated rocks high into the air, before plummeting down once more.

Mist covered the land, blanketing all view of the cliffs. Only baleful red showed where the lava burned.

Coming back to the matter at hand, he buried the hatred again.

He rebuilt his armies and made them more powerful than before.

He needed only one more minion to ensure his victory over L'pilth: The aged Sidhe Queen of the Winter Court.

With her as an undead bound to his will, there would be no power on this side which could hold him back from his plans.

Her time would come as soon as his scout reported where the Winter Court reigned during the height of summer in this region.

"We struck truly. Rathi fell to our fire and winged warriors," Prince Nir insisted.

Princess Jirl giggled, "Rathi has returned from worse wounds with greater power. A little fire does nothing, brother."

Alemific found himself glad his gem eye could not roll. It made it harder for the two vain siblings to see his weariness with their prattles.

Dla'san, Master Ruler of Sla'der, waved his hand dismissively, "Did the hidden spell take?"

"Yes. The ones who fled from his cave reported rivers of blood streaming from the cave when they approached," Nir smirked, "Rathi is fatally wounded."

Jirl twirled, her beaded veil swinging around with a glittering effect, "But he has a knight now. The famed and monstrous Black Knight himself has joined the blood-doffer."

Alemific had not shared the vision he'd gained from the dying bard he'd directed to the most populous village on the border.

The bard had been struck down with a whirlwind akin to the one which sliced through his armies once upon a time.

Then the Black Knight came into view, black armor gilded with blackish green embellishments, visor hiding all identifying marks from view.

The single oddity Alemific saw was a lack of seams or gaps full plate usually bore.

As if the Black Knight had been forged into his armor.

Most would not have caught sight of it, too focused on the mace the Black Knight brought down on their head, but he had seen it.

He recalled tales of a cursed knight, one who in their pride sneered at a master crafter when presented with a suit of armor as a gift.

The armor came to life in defense of its maker, encasing the prideful knight such he could never remove it.

When the knight died, partly from his attempts to break the armor off through battle, the armor moved on, taking on new knights to torment and harry until they returned to the other side.

Perhaps this Black Knight was the latest in a chain of victims.

However, he didn't act like a victim.

If the bard hadn't been so blurry-eyed from his suffering, perhaps Alemific would have gained more insight into this new enemy.

Queen of Eternity, Ingre of Ihovet called order, "While we waste our time here bickering on if Rathi is felled or not, whether this Black Knight is the one of legend or a fake, we are losing our opportunity. We need to march on L'pilth while her king is unable to defend from us. King Ulember, your thoughts?"

Alemific smirked inside at the foolishness of the other rulers. None of them suspected the name he gave them was a false one.

It was best not to show one's cards, especially as Alemific was tied to stories of defeat and the lesson of pride leads afore a disaster.

"Send in the crystal constructs. Only the king has managed to corral them. This Black Knight rides a mortal horse, yes?"

Nir tossed his head imperiously, "Of this, I am certain."

"They cannot travel as fast as Rathi, so we attack from the border of Ihovet. By the time this knight arrives, we will have claimed the territory."

At last the land next to his defeat would be under his control.

Gleeful at victory, he manipulated the other rulers to use their resources in sieging L'pilth.

By the time they realized he overtook their lands with his liches, they would already be bound to him.

Alemific smiled as his blind eye sparkled with the spiderweb of cracks crossing the visible surface.

Xyan stood sentinel at the entrance to her domain.

The rotting corpse deep inside the cavern system did not make her gag nor disturbed, unlike unprepared mortals.

Even if it did, she'd stand guard as she had done for millenniums.

To guard the earthly remains of a once proud and mighty deity.

Like those who helped her gain immortality, she would ensure those bodies in her keeping would decay in peace.

If anyone did manage to overcome her defenses, they would be tracked down and made to suffer for their impudence.

Though, she did wish to have company besides the skeletons she made of ill-fated thieves, and her pets.

The thieves never repented their ways, even after centuries of obeying her commands. A sad fate for those who should know better than to mess with powers beyond their ken.

Snorting out a breath, she watched the forest begin its yearly cycle of losing its colors for more uniform brown.

She never tired of seeing the leaves slowly change through the season, then flutter away when the high winds howled through the hills surrounding her stronghold.

Perhaps some more thieves would challenge her traps and snares to help time progress more swiftly.

She turned her head eyes narrowing on movement in the forest.

Ready to call one of her pets to carry her into battle, she focused a spell into the forest.

Bark became her ears, the dry crackling leaves her eyes, branches her limbs.

She smiled as soon as she realized who travelled in the forest, for they were no threat.

The Court of Summer, headed away from their home when the seasons shifted.

She didn't know where they went, but on occasion over the centuries, a glimpse of them, or their sibling courts, could be made out.

They never offended her sense of duty so she didn't strike out at them.

Something was different this time.

They moved with tension.

As if an enemy stalked them, yet she saw none.

"Will we be called in the middle of our seasonal travel, my Queen?" A nervous guard whispered.

"There is time yet before she may need all of us at vigil. Those who find their end at old age will do so at their heart home. Hers is behind us when winter holds sway."

Xyan frowned, unsure what they talked about.

The tension tightened among their party, rather than ease with the explanation.

Her hearing faintly detected an interloper, so she swung away from the convoy to seek potential prey.

A rotting misshapen creature flapped its oozing wings as it pursued the Court of Summer.

The burning scent of its master permeated the air around it.

Demonic mages never proved a good sign.

She pulled back, then touched her spells, empowering them to the higher levels.

A demonic mage always tried to get to the bodies she stood vigil over.

Never again would she fall for their interests in others.

She had only herself to rely on, unlike last time a demonic mage made off with bits and pieces of a deity.

Her partner left to track the demonic mage down, leaving her as guardian. Only he never returned.

Growling without sound, she prepared for war.

Chapter 16

Revealed

"We come unerringly for you"

Z'ronia waited for the mages and the healers to finish their review of the spell.

For a newly crafted spell from a group, it seemed unnaturally balanced.

Worried they missed something, a side effect or possible disaster, they picked over it one more time.

The Seneschal huffed more the longer it went.

"Are you sure you will bear the brunt of the spell?" Vorbe asked softly.

Z'ronia nodded, "Those who could lessen a side effect cannot cast it, so the healers and mages must stay outside. You would die from casting it like Master Healer Hagh stated, while the others have no magic power but those made for them."

They didn't have time to wait for her to fully recover her magic either. Rathi weakened each minute. She had to risk going unconscious to save the king, as scary and vulnerable it would make her.

"Black Knight?"

Z'ronia walked over to Hagh, then waited for the outcome.

"We suspect there will be at least one side-effect, maybe more. Are you still willing to cast the spell?"

Z'ronia nodded, "I am willing. Are you willing to support me through the side-effect?"

"I'll drag them with me," Hagh sounded like he was smiling, "We will be just outside the door, just in case the spell's drain range is more than a single person."

"Say when you have everyone in place. I'll begin the incantation then," Z'ronia turned towards where the king lay, breaths growing raspier with each exhale.

Hagh told her the room was clear.

Kneeling next to the bed, Z'ronia bowed her head, focusing on the spell, forging the intention as some of the most complex words began forming with her breaths.

Time held still as she spun magic into a new spell.

Gasping breaths chased the words, centering her back into the moment.

Forcing her desire to save Rathi into the spell, offering her magic as tribute, she uttered the final phrase.

One moment she knelt there, the next she stood facing Rathi.

She knew it was Rathi by the taste of the king's skin, the power shivering every muscle in the body as if she'd touched Rathi all over, the scent of leather, rock dust, cedar and old blood. The breathing was far smoother than what she heard.

Pain lashed Z'ronia from where her soul jar nestled.

She grunted, clutching her chest, surprised to find nothing piercing her armor.

Hands gripped her elbows, steadying her as she realized she had been swaying.

Then she knew everything about Rathi.

Her mind filled with memories.

Being chased from a home for being other.

Deciding to be a man when speaking to others.

The bite which stole mortality away.

Mockery as Rathi tried to live among vampires, live up to their standards.

The glorious moment when Rathi's sire died, freeing Rathi to live as she desired.

Coming across minotaurs under siege by human murderers, though the attackers pleaded they were merely poachers.

The rage of killing the poachers so they knew fear as they died.

The oaths of the minotaurs to be Rathi's guards and keepers of the camp.

Deaths and births as Rathi's vassals thrived.

Coming to L'pilth and knowing this was the land to make a home.

Fending off attacks by constructs, carcasses, mages and other enemies.

Winning new allies to join the growing kingdom and becoming dear friends.

The dearest being close to her seat of power.

She ruled without lasting damage.

Until the winged ones struck with some strange weapon which bled Rathi out.

"You have suffered," A strange yet familiar voice jolted Z'ronia from those memories, "Loving family murdered, companions loyal stolen from you, exiled from your kingdom, yet through it all you kept who you are."

Then the agony chased Z'ronia down into darkness, away from Rathi's warm hands.

Hagh held up a hand as the Black Knight collapsed forward.

"Black Knight?" Hagh called.

No movement save for Rathi's chest rising and falling.

The terrible dying gasps had ended.

"Black Knight?" Hagh eased slowly into the room.

The blood orb dropped as Rathi began feeding.

Still the Black Knight didn't make a sound nor motion.

Hagh glanced back, pointed at Vorbe with a glare.

The elderly bard stepped back behind Ghir'ali, gripping his musical instrument with a mulish look on his weathered face.

Moving slowly lest he draw his king's attention, Hagh maneuvered around the bed to the Black Knight's still form.

The king stopped feeding, regaining his color.

Whispering, Hagh placed a hand on the Black Knight's armored shoulder, "Black Knight?"

Nothing.

Casting the assessment spell, Hagh blinked when it was rebuffed by the armor's protections.

Strong protections a master crafter must have died to make.

"I am taking off your helm, Black Knight," Hagh stated gently.

Fearing the side effect had done considerable damage to the knight, Hagh pulled the helm off.

To stare in dismay.

A skull.

Touching the bone, Hagh cast the assessment spell again, dreading what it would tell him.

He held still as he reviewed the spell's outcome.

Female.

Lich.

A very ancient lich, laying unconscious on the king's bed.

The age of the lich practically alarmed Hagh.

Three thousand and seventy nine years as undead.

No years among the living.

Hagh hesitated as the next line filled his mind.

Half of the lich's life energy had been siphoned off from her maximum.

Leaning over so he could touch Rathi's hand, Hagh cast the assessment spell again.

Rathi was whole and hale again, almost bursting with life.

The life from the lich fueled Rathi's recovery.

"Ghir'ali, move slowly to me, left side," Hagh held still, worried the lich may wake at any moment.

Ghir'ali's breath drifted over Hagh's shoulder before the minotaur froze.

"Is that what I think it is?" Ghir'ali rumbled darkly.

"The Black Knight is a lich," Hagh answered softly, barely breathing.

"Our king..."

"Is on the mend. Half the lich's life energy is healing our king. The spell worked."

Ghir'ali sneered, "Put the helm back on."

Hagh fumbled a little but slid it back into place over the skull.

Ghir'ali seized the Black Knight, hefted the armored lich then raced out, snapping the command, "Guard the king."

Vorbe's cry chased the minotaur, "Where are you taking the Black Knight?"

Froda slipped into the room, came closer, "Master?"

"We see to the king," Hagh stated, looking back at his ruler, "There is much we need to do so he wakes quickly."

Chapter 17

Union of Purpose

"Side by side with those souls so true"

Rathi woke slowly, luxuriating in the soft bedsheets.

Voices argued nearby, her Seneschal's and Vorbe's oddly enough.

Vorbe rarely argued with anyone.

Then Rathi recalled the dream she'd just left.

A bent over knight in black armor, who'd lost her family at a young age.

Living happily for years, moving only in the tiny space her father and mother made home.

Losing them to murderers as she hid, trembling.

Grella, the fabled Blue Knight leading her out into the world.

Joy in listening to Grella speak, even the most dry and inane documents.

Then new voices who became her companions.

Rathi realized then she didn't see anything about those companions.

Only heard them, smelled them, touched them and on the rare occasion tasted them.

Then rage and grief as her precious companions began to fall to dagger or sorcery.

Slowly warming to new companions while only Grella remained.

Betrayal and loss.

Exiled from her kingdom for being what she was.

A lich.

Traveling, always alone but for her ever changing mounts.

Hearing the terrible news of Grella falling gravely ill and the shock of knowing her last companion was not long for the other side.

The race back to the kingdom, constant direction spells to try to return to her friend's side as swiftly as possible.

Finding her dear friend lost already before she reached the village Grella called home.

Then bearing vigil for Grella, mourning the only one who'd seen her for who she was.

Z'ronia, guardian, lich, knight, elementalist, honorable.

Rathi slowly sat up, opening her eyes.

She admired her room as if seeing it for the first time.

Z'ronia couldn't see it but she'd focus on the fire crackling in the hearth, the soft whisper of wind through the stone walls, the smell of blood, wood and leather.

One of those early memories radiated through Rathi as the voice of Z'ronia's father explained the world.

"Most beings have five senses: hearing, touch, taste, smell and sight. You were born with only four. Those who have lost their sight or never had it to begin with are called blind. One day, you may be able to see the world, but it will take time, my dear one."

Rathi demanded, "Where is Z...the Black Knight?"

Ghir'ali frowned, "My king, you have just waken from a two day sleep. The knight is dangerous even if you are fully recovered."

"Where?"

Ghir'ali bowed his head, "In the dungeon for mages."

Rathi pulled back the covers, stood from her bed, "Take me to the Black Knight."

Vorbe spoke, "Please allow me to accompany you, King Rathi. The Black Knight knows me far better than your seneschal and you."

A flicker of a blood-frenzy blurred memory made Rathi wince.

Z'ronia keeping Rathi from tearing Vorbe apart to feed, jamming the jaws open with her armored wrist.

"Granted," Rathi moved toward the door, muscles slowly loosening.

Ghir'ali moved with anger as he led the way deep into the mountain.

To the oldest part of Darksteel Keep, where it was said the elementalist who kept a massive army from L'pilth's borders held enemy mages and thieves prisoner.

Z'ronia was kin to the elementalist, so she may be able to escape the dungeon, if she desired it.

They finally arrived to the most secure cell in the entire keep. The one meant to hold demonic mages or angelic mages, indefinitely.

Opening the outer door, Ghir'ali clopped in, gesturing to a minotaur overseeing the cage in the middle of the room.

Rathi knew the returned gesture meant the prisoner had not moved.

Vorbe rushed over to the cage, speaking urgently, "Black Knight?"

Rathi blinked as the helm turned towards Vorbe, a deep voice replying, "Master Bard Vorbe."

"Do you recall what the spell did? Are you injured?"

"The side effect was the transfer of my life energy," the Black Knight explained, "I needed to rest and recover."

Ghir'ali growled, "You are not telling the whole truth."

The helm turned to Ghir'ali as the Black Knight inquired, "What truth do you wish me to share, Seneschal?"

Rathi stepped forward, "Would you remove your helm, without casting the spell to hide your features?"

She knew what would be beneath the helm. A skull with gems taking the place of eyes.

The Black Knight's helm moved as if the lich looked at her, a near perfect mimicry of a sighted person.

Yet Rathi spotted the slight inconsistencies. The visor was slightly lowered and would have blocked the view of the room and Rathi's face. When Z'ronia 'looked' at Vorbe she over compensated, seeming to be looking not at the center of Vorbe's face but maybe his right eye.

"Do you think that is wise, considering what you know of me?"

Rathi smiled glancing at Ghir'ali, "My bloodline's ability allows me to see memories when taking in blood. I never suspected it would apply to life energy."

Ghir'ali's lips pursed.

Vorbe straightened from his lean over, "King Rathi? What is going on?"

Rathi sighed, moving closer to the cage, "Black Knight, please remove your helm. I rather your dear companion knew the real you."

Z'ronia lowered her head, exhaled a breath, as if bracing for ill news.

Then she lifted the helm off.

Vorbe stared at the skull and black gems, just as Rathi did.

Setting the helm down in her lap, Z'ronia turned her head to Vorbe, "I suppose you want the whole tale, Master Bard Vorbe?"

The weariness and defeat in her tone made Rathi tense.

Hopelessness was not her intent in this.

Vorbe smiled, "You have to tell the whole tale from the start. What you turned out to be was third on my list, but on the list."

"Third?" Z'ronia cocked her head.

"Angelic mage and demonic mage beat out lich. Ah, you slipped when talking about the other lich may not be able to overcome your protections."

"So I did," Z'ronia's shoulders slumped, "I was born a lich."

Vorbe sat down, "Born?"

"I had a father and mother. Both were Relic Guardians."

Vorbe perked, "So some still lived."

"I am the last," Z'ronia turned her head to Rathi, "Most liches wouldn't have saved you, King Rathi."

"Most would have known a spell to use rather than cobble one together," Rathi countered.

"Maybe, maybe not. The spell used on you is new or very exotic. Thus the cure had to be new."

Vorbe waved his hands, "I want to know how a lich can be born. Then why your gem eyes are so black and opaque. The stories say lich eyes are translucent."

"No admonishments about raising an undead army?" Z'ronia's voice sounding with a smile the skull didn't display.

"Pfft, you didn't raise one on our journey and you didn't try to kill and make me a part of it. Besides Relic Guardians are known as the Paladins of Artifacts. They usually operated in pairs or solo. Large armies attract attention and lead to the reliquary being pillaged."

"I don't know how my mother or father enabled my birth. My eyes are blind. Lich eyes are supposed to be translucent to allow sight to flow to a lich's spirit. The better cut or clearer the gems, the better their sight," Z'ronia gestured up to her skull, "My mother and father intended to help me replace these darkened gems with clear ones, but they were murdered."

Ghir'ali muttered, "Can't murder the dead."

Rathi sent her seneschal a chiding look, then stepped closer to the cage, "Taking your only chance to see."

Z'ronia nodded, "That is the horrible truth heaped upon their deaths, King Rathi."

Vorbe tapped on the wood of his bassoon, "Did you find justice for your parents?"

"No. I was very young at the time. Grella estimated my age between a thousand and two thousand by the time she found me. They were long dead and their murderers passed to the other side."

Rathi noticed Ghir'ali's tension, faced him.

The minotaur wilted slightly under Rathi's gaze, "Hagh knows his true age."

Z'ronia turned her skull to Ghir'ali, "Hagh knows what I am, then?"

"I'll go get him," Ghir'ali gestured to the minotaurs to watch Rathi's sides, before stomping out.

"Please do not take offense," Rathi started.

Z'ronia made a slicing motion from left to right with two fingers, like a flourish line at the end of a message.

Rathi knew the gesture meant the topic did not need to continue, the grace of it meaning it was alright with Z'ronia.

A tradition specific to Yereen she made without thought.

"So you don't know the real colors of the knights," Vorbe groused suddenly.

Z'ronia cocked her head as she faced Vorbe.

"I wanted to know which hue their armors showed as they charged," Vorbe huffed, "I have to rework the song."

"Your songs are instrumental. How would a color be expressed?"

Laughing Vorbe detailed, "Those of us who master our instruments can have them be just as descriptive with their notes as we are with our voices. It's been ages since I crafted such a song, but it would have told the real tale of Grella and her company."

"A magic infused song," Z'ronia breathed out, "I cannot say their colors or how they looked. I know how they all sounded as they readied weapons, their scents changing as the thunder of hooves led us into enemies, their voices raised in victory or despair."

Vorbe perked, "Tell me that."

Rathi could tell Z'ronia did not know how to react to such an eager request.

"He will pester you until he gets what he wants," Rathi smiled, stroking her beard, "It's why he can get through the Boundary without dying. The songs draw him to safety."

"I would argue his determination to find the most exotic story is what carries him through trials and fire," Z'ronia's voice took on a teasing edge.

Vorbe leaned forward, "Describe a charge."

Rathi listened as she waited for Hagh to return.

With his experience, Vorbe asked questions at key moments, drawing out Z'ronia's perception...awareness of the world.

Hagh inhaled as he entered, "My king?"

"We are curious as to the true age of this knight," Rathi nodded to Z'ronia who'd fallen silent.

Hagh nervously played with his amulet, "Three thousand and seventy nine years as undead, no years as a living being."

Z'ronia touched her skull with her gauntlet, "That old?"

Hagh dropped his hands to his sides, "You didn't know?"

Z'ronia replied, "Time in the cave my family called home meant nothing to me."

"Without sight, time would pass faster," Rathi commented.

"Without sight?" Hagh looked at Z'ronia, "The assessment spell did not show an injury to your eyes."

Z'ronia's voice warmed, "Grella found it odd spells never showed I was injured like those whose sight was taken from them. As if I am how I am meant to be. The only ones who could maybe give me sight are more likely to attack me, either for being a lich, or to make me a minion under their command, so there is no point in trying for a miracle."

Rathi felt all the memories of Grella reading to Z'ronia flow by, countless sessions to help Z'ronia act like someone who had sight, casting illusion spells until her skull didn't show should she have to take her helm off, crafting her armor so she didn't need to take it off.

Years of methods to make Z'ronia not only a capable warrior, but she could navigate the world without help.

"Grella knew you'd out live her," Rathi realized.

Z'ronia stilled, her voice deepening with sadness, "Yes."

Rathi knew the grief still crashing over the lich, aching loneliness as the companions she relied on and who relied on her rode to the other side without her.

Rathi knew that pain, dear friends and lovers passing on, while she remained behind. Almost cursed to a lonely path.

No.

She wasn't alone in this long life anymore.

Z'ronia came riding this far north to find a home.

One she'd never be chased from.

Rathi opened her mouth to speak, but Hagh interrupted, "I hope I have not offended you, Black Knight."

Z'ronia asked, "Why would I be offended?"

"I pulled off your helm without your permission."

"Did you remove it to check my health?"

"Yes," Hagh worried his amulet.

"There is no offense given. I take it I collapsed once the spell finished its work?"

Hagh exhaled in relief, "Yes. You didn't answer and lay so still. I feared you had died to bring our king back."

Z'ronia stiffened, her head turning.

Vorbe asked, "The sentinel spell?"

"Yes," Z'ronia turned to Rathi, then pointed, "That way."

Seeing Ghir'ali's grip on his bow, Rathi asked, "Please stay here. I will attend to the incursion. Ghir'ali."

She walked out, moving up to an exit.

"My king, this lich is a threat to our people."

"So am I. I would have killed Vorbe if the Black Knight hadn't stepped between us," she stopped in the hall, faced her seneschal, "I know every memory he has. Every thought and emotion up to the point he cast the spell to save me. He knows me in return. We both are the same type of men."

Rathi made sure the final word had extra emphasis.

His eyes widened as he whispered, "He is like you?"

"We both move in this world as men, yet are not good enough. He knew love of family, of friends, of companions as a man. Until I met your ancestors, no one did the same for me. Like a reflection on the water, we both are similar but for the waves between us. The Black Knight is as honorable as you. Once a people are under his care, he will move the world to protect them. I suggest you work with him."

"Work with him?"

"The Black Knight is my knight during the times I can't meet our enemies," she smiled viciously, "I pity the other kingdoms. They'll waste so much to try entering our kingdom going forward."

"My king. This...knight could have hidden something from you."

Rathi swung open the doors, relishing the night sky before turning to her seneschal.

"I didn't know any of the knights before at all and they fled due to my vampiric nature," she held up a hand, "I wager three barrels of the apple cider this knight will be the one who stays, in spite of your attempts to drive him off."

Ghir'ali moved his jaw side to side, "Make it seven."

"Four, since I know you'll do your best to get the Black Knight to leave."

"Six," Ghir'ali folded his arms, careful of his bow, "We will have a party when the knight leaves."

"Five and new bardings for all your moose," Rathi accepted his nod, splitting into her flock.

She winged towards her new enemy, eager to tear them into little bits for the near successful assassination, and daring to invade her land.

Vorbe delighted in speaking with the Black Knight, teasing out more and more tales.

This version of the Black Knight, the one who didn't hide who he was made some of the quirky tales more sensical.

The Black Knight who pulled an injured Maroon Knight from a battlefield, all the while holding off marauding hordes. The Black Knight and the Maroon Knight were said to be dire enemies within the company.

A laughing Black Knight who'd participated in drinking games, but never being too drunk to watch out... be alert for danger.

Relaxed in the company of those who knew the real Black Knight and didn't fear the face of undeath before them.

Grella must have loved the time spent alone with the lich.

No others near to judge them.

Sessions of reading out loud the books Grella poured over, seeking some truth others missed.

Hagh slowly warmed to the Black Knight, asking questions after some time.

Like did food just fall through the bones?

"The food is consumed, but I do not gain any energy from it. I do enjoy tasting food and beverages. Though travel rations are merely tolerated."

Was it true animals ran in fear on meeting her?

Vorbe didn't react on finding out his companion wasn't a male lich, too enthralled to mind the new information.

"Animals are sensitive to my presence, though their reactions vary. Horses tend to have one of two reactions: Stark fear or intense glee."

Vorbe straightened, "Plodder is one of the latter?"

"Yes, and every mount I've ridden. Grella was quite embarrassed her original mount refused to go near me. Even swathed in the most foul smelling leathers and robes she could find, her horse would bolt if I drew too close. She spent much to find two horses who'd let me be near them. Then she began breeding them in the hope she'd have a herd for new knights. Unfortunately, about half didn't like me."

After a few hours she paused, then added, "The sentinel spell has gone silent."

"Then our king has made swift work of the enemy," Hagh heaved a sigh of relief.

"What sort of enemies attack?" The Black Knight asked.

"I think the minotaurs or the king can answer that better than I," Hagh stated.

"You have to heal wounds made by the attackers. That information can be very valuable," The Black Knight countered, "Certain enemies make the same type of attacks until a defense is put in place to prevent it. Knowing where they strike can lead a blacksmith or a master crafter to forge a parry or block."

Hagh frowned, "The ones who arrive from construct attacks almost to the last look like some great beast mauled them. Slashing, goring, tearing mostly, though there was one time we got someone who'd been crushed, like a snake had wrapped, then squeezed them. The armored attacks are mostly crushing and slashing. Jagged swords based on the bits I've pulled from wounds."

The Black Knight asked, "Why armored?"

"Oh, they are like you, fully armored. The one time we tried to spare one, we couldn't open the armor to get at the wounds. The armor is poured unto their skin so it's melded to them. It may explain their gibbering madness when they attack."

"My armor is not melded to me as it would reduce my mobility. Their armor resisted all attempts to breach it?"

Hagh blew out a breath, "Took acid and hours of work to peel it open. That was after the armored individual died. Finely crafted by a master blacksmith, though I loath the way they applied it."

"What other enemies are there?"

"Lots of different assassination groups, usually dealt with by our king. A few thieves, though they focus mostly on bodies to take with them. A couple demonic mages often enough I need to have burn salves stocked all the time."

"What group would winged individuals belong?" The Black Knight asked.

"Were they armored all over? They could be with the kingdom that has the armored attacks."

Vorbe offered, "Just the wings were metal. They wore leathers as armor."

"Maybe the thieves or assassins, then?" Hagh blew out a breath, shrugged, "I really can't tell."

"An array of enemies, with some that may coordinate with each other, or compete with one another," the Black Knight murmured, "This has been helpful."

"How?" Hagh demanded.

"Constructs require large amounts of magic to build and maintain. Destruction would drain the enemy over time. To counter armored attacks we need a weapon which can cut through the plates or immobilize the enemies so they cannot harm anyone. Assassins and thieves need ways in and out. Find the tunnels and holes they use, guard them with the intention of removing them after cornering the enemy. The winged ones can be brought down by one of my spells with rather fatal results, but with leather only, they could be felled by arrows, especially those wielded by the minotaurs."

Vorbe hid a smile as one of the minotaurs challenged, "We only have axes."

"I can smell the wood, the oiled string and the arrows' feathers. Duck feathers based on how they are brushing one another in your quiver."

The minotaur's ears lowered, "You can tell all that?"

The Black Knight nodded, "I can. I also know you have a wooden hafted weapon of some weight at your belt, either secured by a chain or a chain is part of it. If part of it, it would be a flail of some type. If secured, it must have more weight to it since leather can't hold it."

Vorbe looked at the minotaur's side then replied, "Ball and chain. A very useful weapon in a fight, as is your skill to identify from an array of signs."

"Sometimes. However in combat there can be so many noises and smells that the signs can be lost. Hence the need for full armor and magic enhancements to said armor," The Black Knight seemed to look down through the floor to some incomprehensible vision, "I've been saved more by the sensation of wind moving around me, or the ground vibrating than by scent or sound."

"If there are quiet moments," Rathi's voice jolted Vorbe and Hagh, "would you play games?"

The Black Knight seemed to give a rueful expression, "Most games I am able to play, I cannot be the dealer for."

"I'm sure I could persuade Vorbe to assist with that. It wouldn't do for me to be dealer either, considering I know how you can tell your cards," Rathi held up a hand to Ghir'ali, "Besides, Hagh and Vorbe need better seats than the floor so they can continue this discussion."

Ghir'ali grumbled something under his breath, then unlocked the cage.

The Black Knight asked, "Would it be possible to see to Plodder before we play? I fear he may be a little disturbed by my absence."

"I'm curious what Plodder makes of vampires," Rathi's smile seemed more relaxed than last Vorbe beheld it.

The Black Knight put her helm back on, stood slowly, "I have crossed paths with a few vampires. Those do not cause the same reaction as a lich does. However, I haven't run into a vampire with Plodder yet, so his reaction may be different."

Vorbe stretched then stood, walking beside the Black Knight as they all exited the dungeon, "So, what weapons do I bear?"

The Black Knight gave a hum, "Three daggers or short swords wrapped with some strange leather, covered in an odd oil. Some tangy metal coil along with wood. Seems like a weapon used on me by an assassin that Grella called a garrote. It scratched my armor, last I fell victim to an attack. A wood club with hemp and leather. Then most importantly your bassoon, drum and...," The Black Knight paused, "The jangling one you gave me. It's still tied to Plodder."

"It's a tambourine," Vorbe chuckled, "Why most importantly?"

"You are a bard. Your instruments have magical power as do you. In Yereen, bards were divested of their instruments, gagged and bound so they couldn't muster their magics."

"You did that often?"

"I know because they did it fairly often to Ophielen, even though she wasn't a bard. She joked they did it because it was the only way they could catch a woman."

Vorbe laughed, "I do want to listen to more stories about all the colorful knights from Grella's company. So few are told beside Grella, you, the red knight and the gray knight."

The Black Knight's demeanor turned as black as her armor, "I had hoped the Gray Knight's tale had been forgotten."

"The famous betrayer will always be found in a tale," Vorbe hesitated, "especially with the end she found, hung by her own rope off the tower she intended the young prince to die from."

"The end she found wasn't the one told of," the Black Knight seemed to draw back the aura, "She became something most foul before she was sent to the other side."

"What did she become?" Vorbe dared to ask.

"A demoness. She didn't figure I'd find out she lived and was determined to take the price of her traitorous acts out of her hide. It took years to find her."

"Was that when you parted ways with Grella."

"After I left Grella. All the tales said the Gray Knight was dead, so many began to question my youth compared to Grella, as the last two remaining knights. She sent me away. I began hearing of a ghostly knight roaming far east of Yereen. I trailed after the ghost until I found the Gray Knight alive and feasting on the misery of a large city. She was very surprised her new spells did not harm me."

"You ended her like you did those flyers in the canyon?"

"No. I did something far, far worse to the fiend than anyone else suffered at my words or hand," the Black Knight continued up the stairs, ignoring all of Vorbe's pleas to know what happened.

Chapter 18

Freedom from Oppression

"Our duty unwinds before us"

Z'ronia fell easily into a pattern with Rathi.

During daylight hours, she rode out with Plodder, using the magical paths to dash across the land in minutes rather than days.

At night, Rathi would join in, crossing paths as they both moved about, dealing with threats from the other side of the Boundary or those internal to L'pilth.

When the nights were quiet, they would set up in the hall and play games where she could participate using touch and hearing.

She'd keep an ear out for the sentinel spell as it always alerted someone crossing into the land with nefarious deeds in mind.

Vorbe instructed the local bards of songs beyond the Boundary, sharing distant lands, peoples, and wars.

Z'ronia liked the quiet nights best, even with the overbearing presence of Ghir'ali, Rathi's seneschal.

Picking up the cards, feeling the markings Grella had helped her craft unto the deck, she discovered she obtained the balanced elements hand.

Grella found the Deck of Distant Lands and insisted everyone learn it, only because the types fit Z'ronia's spells or the minions they faced as a company.

Fire, Water, Earth, Air, Life and Death cards graced her hand.

The only one more powerful was the arranged forces: Vampire, Lich, Demon, Angel, Deity, The Other Side.

Grella loved declaring her hand, fanning it out so the marked cards made a small noise, each one slightly different.

A habit Rathi picked up quickly to Z'ronia's enjoyment.

"I declare my hand ready," Rathi formally stated.

"I find myself at that point as well," Z'ronia countered with the equally formal response.

"The beast dens," Rathi flared the cards, letting Z'ronia confirm the cards were correct: Wolfen, Dire Serpent, Eclipse Hawk, Kraken, Lavamander, Moontusk.

"The balanced elements," Z'ronia fanned out her cards, making sure they showed.

Rathi laughed, filling the hall with warmth, "I am bested."

Z'ronia inclined her helm, "For now. Like before, you may be next to win."

A strange tolling of bells sounded from the sentinel spell, making Z'ronia listen carefully.

"Another enemy?" Rathi asked.

"Not the enemy warning this time," she tapped into the web of spells the last elementalist laid, seeking what the bells meant.

"Someone crossing, but not an enemy," Z'ronia turned her helm to Rathi, "Powerful individuals. At harmony with the land, per the spells information."

Rathi perked, "Ah. The Spring Court must have arrived."

An alarm overlaid the bells, making Z'ronia growl, "Dy'wanei side again."

"This is their fifth attempt this week. Go deal with them. I'll handle our sidhe guests."

Z'ronia left the deck of cards on the table, rising to her feet before bowing to Rathi.

Then using the earth paths inside Darksteel Keep, she moved through the stone to the stables, not needing to take a step to find herself where she needed to go.

"Plodder, come," she ordered, opening the door for her mount's stall.

He snorted, trotting out.

She mounted, then accessed the earth paths again, bringing Plodder with her.

As long as she stayed inside the sentinel spell's range, the earth paths willingly accepted her and Plodder moving throughout the land with ease. She found out there were offshoots of the earth paths spreading out beyond, but they were not as well kept or smooth as those inside L'pilth. On one rather slow day, she'd managed to use the paths to hop across the entire kingdom of Laeb East to reach the edge of the Free Trade Zone.

She knew it because Vorbe had led her past a distinctive landmark: A whistling hole which never varied through the seasons, per Vorbe's stories.

Coming back had taken a while, but she'd managed it in time to intercept an incoming force, landing among them before they got any where near a village.

Plodder tossed his head.

"I know you do not like the earth paths. They get us where we need to faster. Which means faster back to your hay and water," she replied gently.

Plodder clopped out of the rocky niche, snorting unhappily.

Navigating by sound and the elementalist spells made the journey faster.

They came to stop before the village, turned to where the enemy would approach.

A bend ahead would give the enemy little warning before they were nearly on top of Z'ronia and Plodder.

However, she could hear them, their heavy footsteps echoing along the walls.

The sounds reminded her of her home, where she could hear her mother approaching long before she could be hugged.

Except this time she would be sending these interlopers to the other side and the Grasp's embrace.

"We stealing?" A voice asked, the echo faint to Z'ronia's ears.

"Steal head healer village. Make carcass. Master happy."

Z'ronia figured one of the leaders of Dy'wanei must be a demonic mage at the very least. They always went after the villagers who possessed powers or special abilities.

Those people tended to make the best carcasses, corpse hunters, or the winged creatures. Their inherit power became their prison until someone managed to destroy the bodies enough to send them to the other side.

Wind ahead of Plodder shifted, signaling her opponents were turning the bend.

A snort, then mockery, "Small black thing."

Giants, Z'ronia surmised based on the comment and how much wind they blocked.

"Who are you?" She challenged, mentally pulling up the list of giants Rathi asked her to offer a change of sides.

"Small black thing with big voice," the voice huffed in disdain, "Joit's foot smash."

Z'ronia called the rocks to unbalance the giant, recognizing the name as one Rathi wanted to tempt over.

Joit and his partner, Kump, where nomads before Dy'wanei enslaved them. They usually cleared rocks and hauled them to areas where they could build villages or other things.

The land shook as the giant hit the ground.

"Small thing is Black Knight," she stated clearly.

"You kill cackle cackle?" Joit asked.

"Who or what is cackle cackle?" Z'ronia didn't know what Joit meant.

There was movement then she got the impression the giant was leaning into her space, "Flying cackle cackle. Call us stupid. Master say you smash from air. Make cackle cackle more smushed smushed."

Z'ronia realized he meant the smiling voiced flyer she'd inadvertently crushed into the ground with her empowered chant, "Well cackle cackle was a bit rude. I don't accept rudeness."

Joit laughed, voice booming off the canyon walls, "You funny small Black Knight."

Kump snorted, "We need healer."

Joit sighed, "Kump right. Master mean if no healer."

"What does this master hold over you, Joit?"

"Bad collar. Collar no come off. Whip hurt too," Joit groused.

Z'ronia breathed a spell to tell her what magic items were around her.

While specialized, it would give her an idea of what the collar did.

Only she felt no magic before her. The only magic item was behind her in the village.

"I don't sense magic in the collar," she stated.

"No magic. Blacksmiths stronger than Joit. Stronger than mate Kump."

She dismounted from Plodder, "Lean down and I will assess if I can remove the collars. If I can, King Rathi wishes to speak with you."

"What blood-doffer want?" Kump asked.

Laying her hands on Joit's collar, she whispered a spell to touch all surfaces of it.

Grella taught her this variation so she could understand an object a sighted person could from looking it over.

A seamless band circled the giant's neck.

She had a bad feeling as she investigated further.

It proved true as she found the collar forged into the skin of Joit.

"Did the blacksmith pour molten metal over your neck?"

"Hurt bad. No move. Then chain put on. Made to be dogs," Kump whined.

"Who held you?" She asked, pondering steps to reverse how the collar was formed, or free the giants.

"Cracked eye skull. Skull scary."

"A skeleton?" She asked, hoping to keep them talking.

Rathi may send one of her owl forms over to see what happened, just in case Z'ronia needed help with the local villagers.

Not all of them knew of Z'ronia yet, or didn't trust her.

"Sparkling eye. Smell bleh."

"Sparkling eye as in gem eye?" She asked urgently.

"Yes. Mean gem eye. Cracked dead other eye."

A lich in Dy'wanei. That didn't bode well in her estimate. She'd speak privately with Rathi.

"Joit," Rathi's voice rang out as wingbeats sounded overhead, "Kump. Welcome to L'pilth."

"Small bird know us?" Joit sounded amazed.

"Small bird is King Rathi, or at least a part of him," Z'ronia stated, "King Rathi, their collars have been poured unto them. I believe I need Hagh's expertise to remove them without harming Joit and Kump."

"No magic in the collars?" Rathi seemed suspicious.

"Not per my spells."

"May I?" Rathi asked.

Z'ronia bowed her helm, "As you wish, King Rathi."

The scent of blood filled the air briefly, a shiver of magic ghosting over Z'ronia's armor like a fine vibration when it briefly stroked across the magic imbued in the metal.

"It's subtle, but not magic in the traditional sense. There's a suggestion in their minds."

"Suggestion?" Z'ronia heard once some bards and those with demonic or vampiric heritages could induce someone to act outside their norm.

Most used it to seduce a desired bed partner to adult activities. Ophielen supposedly had the capability, since she attracted attention wherever she travelled.

"Vorbe will need to aid in this," Rathi sighed, "Follow my Black Knight. He will lead you to my keep, Joit, Kump."

Z'ronia led the two giants to Darksteel Keep, Rathi flying overhead as they made their way through the canyons.

Whispering the spell so she could speak with Rathi far overhead, she asked, "The Court of Spring?"

"I am escorting them in. They'll arrive before Joit and Kump. Perhaps if Hagh, Vorbe, you and I are unable to relinquish the suggestions hold, they may assist, for a few kegs of my maple infused mountain spring water."

Z'ronia smiled, "Ah, so they are one of your friends you build your stockpile for."

"Considering how you enjoy it as well, I will be ensuring I have plenty for a long siege."

Z'ronia grinned at the teasing note in Rathi's voice, "Just as I am creating all those candies you find pleasing."

"Ah, that's right, you can make those without aid of a kitchen. I would be remiss if I didn't ask you to supply some of your simpler recipes to my cooks," Rathi purred.

Z'ronia thanked Grella for being so free with exploring topics, including esoteric ones. She'd been the one to come across the candies and meals fit for various monsters, chief among them vampires.

The candies also could be used as a sort of field ration for vampires without regular donors or a blood orb like Rathi possessed.

They spoke as they led two possible new citizens to the keep.

The Queen of the Spring Court watched Rathi take human form, floating to the ground as a black clad knight riding a war horse in black barding led two giants up the twisting path to the doors of Darksteel Keep.

He turned to his fellow co-ruler, smiled, "Notice it?"

The King of the Spring Court grinned, "Now isn't that interesting."

Both sidhe men watched King Rathi interact with the knight and the two giants.

"Ah, those two are Joit and Kump," the Queen of Spring leaned on the banister, looking down on the towering forms, "It's been ages since they stomped through our home territories looking for food. A bit thin and raggedy, but easily beefed up with some care. The knight though..."

The King of Spring nodded, "Never seen Rathi act that way with one of his knights before. Nor a knight react like that. It's more than friendly."

"As if they are in the season of new lovers," The Queen leaned on his hand, "Usually at this phase in Rathi's pursuit, the lover-to-be either runs or is very nervous. This one is tranquil by comparison. Look!"

They watched Rathi touch the knight's elbow, hand lingering a mite longer than a king to loyal knight would.

The two sidhe hummed, eagerly observing.

"The Winter Court didn't note a lover, in or out of armor," the Queen of Spring side-glanced at his peer, "We must be the first."

"This happened rather quickly," The King of Spring nodded, "The knight must have allowed Rathi to drink from him. Rathi would know everything about the knight."

"The knight is acting like he's been in Rathi's service for years. Maybe some clairvoyance or its kin? Look, they move as one," the

Queen of Spring's grin widened further, "We are not the only ones to spot it. Twenty dewed flowers the seneschal is trying to break them up."

Ghir'ali's scowl practically scorched the knight as he stomped over, Hagh and Vorbe in his wake.

"Too easy, so we'll exchange ten dewed flowers. I have some vibrant blue ones if you are willing to part with those deep purple ones," the King of Spring cocked his head, "The feeling is reciprocated at least, based on the tone in the knight's voice."

The Queen jabbed the King's side, "I don't have the same hearing range as you."

"You make up for it with your greater vision. I get the feeling Ghir'ali has walked in on the two enjoying far less discreet activities than caresses, based on how he just stepped between them," the King gestured to one of the waiting servants, requested a jug of apple cider and two mugs.

"He's not acting out of jealousy, so that's good for Rathi's court. Remember that lovely minotaur with the fluffy hooves? She did not like anyone getting near her master," the Queen snorted watching the group below with amusement.

"She did that because one of Rathi's former lovers almost killed him after a pleasant night in bed. She took personal offense anyone would dare to assassinate her king. As I recall she didn't like you."

"I did try to bed Rathi, but he turned me down with such grace, I could only be his friend going forward," The Queen of Spring pointed, "Spells and armor. Nice combination, especially if he has a sharp mind to pair with them. Rathi certainly got himself a very good catch there."

The King of Spring pondered the black knight below, "Perhaps too good?"

"Want me to accidentally knock his helm off, or trip him?" The mischievous smirk vanished as quickly as it appeared.

"I want to see how the knight reacts to standing guard with ours. Could be a bigot like that one a century and a quarter ago who hated sidhe with a vengeance."

"I'll mention it to Ghir'ali when I see if some stews can be made from the venison we brought with us for the morrow's meal," the Queen straightened, whispering, "If this knight is a threat?"

"We ensure the threat is short lived," the King replied softly, then smiled as the servant handed them mugs, a jug, before bowing themselves back inside, "Let's go inside and linger over Rathi's excellent cider while they work on those ugly collars."

They swept inside as the group below worked on removing the bindings from the two giants.

Chapter 19

Glimpses

"To glorious and distant horizons"

He waited at the landing impatiently, eager to return to the spot bards and other artists entered so he could gather all the songs, dances, and arts he missed being here, where he shouldn't have ended up in the first place. At least not for several centuries considering the care he took with his well-being.

It had just been his luck to be within range of that horrid spell when it got cast.

To end up here and unable to return, unless another lich, maybe a vampire with innate magic abilities, could cast the spell to get here then have the mental fortitude to return.

Leaving him at the beck and call of one he shouldn't have to obey for a long while. He should be over there gathering dances and songs to delight or horrify people.

He sighed, then couldn't stand still a moment longer.

Listening to music only he could hear, he began moving, his dancing outfit flittering with his moves, flaring out the beaded fringes as the bells chimed on his boots and hood.

The mosaic glass covering his face sparkled as light crossed his vision, allowing him to see outward, but no one to see his face.

Relaxing into the twirls, leaps and sweeps, he expressed his frustrations and desires across the landing.

"While I find your dances intriguing, I would ask you to halt for a time, Master Bard Nilian," the voice stopped the music in his mind as surely as a band stopping at a lord's command.

Nilian turned to the deity, folded his arms, the bells chiming angrily, "Not like I can do anything when you sever the music in my head like that."

"Would you go recite the latest tales of the Black Knight to S'waliat and C'rorvent? I believe they need the bolster as the eddies form," the deity looked up with resignation, "This time is usually hard on them."

"Why is this time rough for them?" Nilian ventured with more bravado than he felt.

"It is the anniversary of their deaths and separation from their most precious family member. Your stories will cheer them until the eddies calm."

Nilian considered the deity then asked the question which pestered him for millenniums, "Are the eddies related to their moods?"

The deity shook its head, "No, the eddies are a result of their untimely demise. They were meant to live for another six thousand years. Someone intervened and disrupted the balance between life, death, and undeath. Just like the eddies form on the day you and those who came with that spell so long ago."

Nilian straightened, "What do you mean?"

"The caster was weakened intentionally so they couldn't return with those who passed the trials," the deity looked up, "Only a catastrophic event could have cracked the foundation of that lich's mind, or the intervention from one of the other planes."

"He blames himself for not being able to return and the only catastrophe was not being able to return with all his successful students," Nilian looked back to the center market where he'd crossed paths with the ill-spirited lich earlier, "Angels know those types are forces for good against the endless spawn of the befouled ones."

"You have come to the same conclusion I have. A demon or demon spawn up there has been carefully building this plan, taking out liches who would contest their reign or schemes. Only three remain opposite the befouled ones: a deity-watcher, a relic-keeper, and a child of the Grasper line."

Nilian looked upward, then huffed a breath he didn't need, "So why do tales of the Black Knight help?"

"Because the Black Knight is the child of the Grasper line," the deity smiled, "My most devoted and lawful of the undead served under that line."

Nilian pieced it together then why the two liches who'd been crushed to death by villagers needed the stories.

"You better note down all," Nilian reiterated the last word again, "of the songs and dances I'll miss collecting during my performance."

The deity spoke with a sort of dreamy distraction which meant it looked to the other side, leaving the shell of its body behind, "See my vassal. She will have your price waiting."

Nilian took that as dismissal and walked off to fulfill his duty.

To lift morale for his allies, and decimate the wills of his enemies, he would cross wits with even the deity behind him with vigor and a forceful tone.

Stepping off the landing, he ghosted across the air towards the distant home of those who'd meet their final death and had no ability to return to the other side.

Rathi hid the smile on her face as Z'ronia joined the guards at the wall, Ghir'ali looking like a trap had been sprung.

The King and Queen of Spring sipped cider as they played a tri-player game from their game-masters called Trials of the Shadows.

Whoever managed to get the card for Consuming Shadows, won the game. However, there were cards to prevent the card from showing up via magic the game-masters imbued the set with.

It was a pity Z'ronia couldn't play. The deck was so visually based with no markings to help her read the cards.

"So you are the original Black Knight?" One of the guards of Spring inquired politely.

Z'ronia's deep voice filled Rathi with delightful shivers, "I was honored to ride with the Blue Knight from the start."

"Must have been very young to still have strength to wield the sledge hammer now," the guard replied.

"Being young at spirit provides enough strength to match my foes." Chuckles rounded the room.

Rathi played a card listening as the guard and Z'ronia spoke about various topics, from weapons, mounts, armor, fighting in different seasons and terrains.

If Rathi hadn't been aware of Z'ronia's blindness, her answers kept it entirely hidden.

"You win," the King of Spring chortled.

Rathi looked down, snorted as she realized she laid down the Consuming Shadows card, "So I have."

"I swear you are tactically superior when you aren't thinking about it," the Queen of Spring gathered the cards, shuffled them absently, "Though I hope it is more than armor admiration."

Rathi leaned forward, lowering her voice, "You know I've never been one for outward appearances, just like you and your consort, dear Queen."

"The armor helped seal the deal, though," the Queen laughed, his smile widening, "I thought her too good to be true at the time."

Rathi smirked at the insinuation and subtle question, "You know my abilities make lies very hard to hide when given my time to explore the spirit."

"True. You did help us with the suspected traitors and found they both were, just in different ways," the King of Spring leaned in, "So does the dungeon match the keep walls?"

Rathi guffawed, "That has made the rounds already?"

"Indeed," the King of Spring tilted his head to Z'ronia, "So does it?"

"Hmm," Rathi picked up the cards the Queen of Spring dealt, intentionally teasing the two sidhe monarchs.

Z'ronia called out then, "Boundary crossing. I'll deal with them."

"If it's near Hijort, please pick up their shipment of bark," Rathi replied, reviewing her cards.

"Even if it isn't, I'll collect the shipment, King Rathi," Z'ronia vanished using the earthpath spell the keep supported.

"An Elementalist?" The King of Spring looked at Rathi with appreciation, "A capable ally considering the land here."

"The Black Knight is far more than his armor shows," Rathi laid down the Consuming Shadows card, "Seems my luck in this hand came at the start."

"I did ask the gamemasters to allow it to show randomly in hands," the Queen of Spring sat back, "Your knight doesn't mind sidhe, giants, nor minotaurs. Any he disagrees with?"

"Demonic mages, liches, and oath breakers," Rathi replied, recalling the memories carved with burning hatred.

"That goes without saying," the King of Spring chided, "Truly, does he seek harm outside of those?"

Rathi gathered the cards, shuffling them, considering the question as seriously as the two sidhe meant it to be, "Those who harm his allies and wards. There is little the Black Knight would not do to pursue those who cross that line and make them pay."

Vorbe walked in with the local bards, began setting up.

"One more hand before the night's entertainment begins?" Rathi slid cards across at the two nods.

They played cards, delaying the appearance of the Consuming Shadows card, listening idly as the bards began tuning their instruments for their song.

The ground rumbled, shaking everything.

Rathi sighed, "Hmm, the Black Knight found another spell to adjust."

"Spell?" The Queen of Spring looked alarmed.

"The land helps all elemental spells, and the Black Knight is very powerful to begin with. Ghir'ali can attest to the results of a low level tornado spell being cast here by an elementalist. I wager it was a collection of constructs he dispatched."

The King of Spring considered Rathi then offered, "Two bushels of sweetgrass he dispatched a living army of invaders."

Not to be outdone the Queen of Spring added, "Three barrels of thaw fish, he just attended to another set of giants."

Rathi slid the cards out for the next round, "If I'm accurate, I get one new game that relies on sounds to be played, from each and every one of your gamemasters. If not, you can have half the maple infused mountain spring water in my cellar."

The King played the Consuming Shadows card, "I look forward to finding out. I win."

Vorbe gestured to the bards, the beginning strains filling the air.

His bassoon joined in, the magic coalescing around the artists.

The spell beckoned the listener to close their eyes.

Rathi submitted, relaxing to enjoy the music.

Instead, she felt the muscles of a horse between her thighs, the clop of hooves thundering over ground, the creak of leather, flapping of cloaks and banners.

Voices calling back and forth, urging greater speed and to meet the enemy with force.

War horns rang challenge across the land.

A clarion voice bellowing, "For Yereen!"

Rathi felt her voice joining others, becoming the war cry of the charge.

Warm air sliced by with the scent of smoke, cooked flesh, blood and split organs, filling her with almost unspeakable rage.

Rathi felt as if she was both in the song and part of the memory it came from as Z'ronia's thoughts overlaid reality from a long ago battle.

Then metal gripped her shoulder, pulling her out of the horrid memory, muting it so she could enjoy the music.

The excitement echoed around her as the company clashed with rivals, horses trumpeting or screaming, clangs of metal on metal, then the rattling strike on her armor as a lucky blow worked through her defenses.

Then the bellows for retreat as the enemy ran.

The joy in defending her company, her kingdom from interlopers filled her, then ebbed as the music drew to a close.

Rathi reached up, covered the gauntlet, opening her eyes before looking up.

Z'ronia stood there, a box tied at her hip, standing as if she never left.

Vorbe stood, his voice filling the silence, "The Knights of Yereen in a Night Charge."

The King of Spring rapped his knuckles on the table, the highest favor from a sidhe to an artist, "I have never experienced a song like that. I believe my bards will want a copy."

Vorbe walked to them, pulling out two scroll tubes, "One for your bards and one for the library."

The King of Spring passed one to the Queen of Spring, took the second, "That must be the work of a lifetime."

Vorbe chuckled, "No, I think I have some better coming still."

"I eagerly await the next one," the King of Spring bowed his head respectfully.

Rathi blinked as Z'ronia pulled out a stone wrapped in metal, presented it to Vorbe.

The sad smile faded to pure joy as Vorbe accepted the token, "Did you buy a bag of the tokens?"

"I did though those were used long ago. Since then I craft my own, applying the same spell those in Impolin used to bless the tokens," Z'ronia replied calmly.

Vorbe looked up in surprise, "Is this your own?"

"Yes. I was told if a master of tokens gifted it, it signaled great appreciation of a fellow master artisan."

Rathi watched the war of grief and love on Vorbe's face, "I accept in the vein it is offered."

Z'ronia turned to Rathi, removing her gauntlet from Rathi's shoulder, "Hijort reports a fungus is attacking their trees. They sent a sample for review. To whom should it be taken?"

Rathi knew Z'ronia memorized the names having been so imbedded in each other memories, so she figured the lich did it to help explain why she returned to Rathi's side.

"To the mages in the lowest level. They'll find a cure," Rathi asked as Z'ronia turned, "So what enemy caused you to use one of your normal spells?"

"Twenty constructs. I haven't had time to adjust the higher level spells as yet. I apologize for the earthquake, King Rathi."

"Are all constructs destroyed?"

"Yes. They were crystalline so I collected the powdery remains. I remember a spell that may be able to make use of the powder. Additionally, those controlling the constructs reclaimed the magic. That would not return much magic to them. They must be desperate for scraps of magic to attempt reclaiming."

Rathi knew the spell she was thinking of, "If the powder works with the spell, make sure the mages get it. We have barrels of the powder around the kingdom that could be made of use."

"King Rathi," the Black Knight departed.

"Well, we have a sound based game to request of our gamemasters," The King of Spring, "The bushels will be handed over from our wagons by morning."

The Queen nodded, his smile widening, "I'll add the thaw fish at the same time.

They began another game, discussing mundane topics.

Chapter 20

Dread

"As stars swirl above in their endless cycles" Siolobha fretted.

Travel had been slowed to a crawl as they fought to get the Queen of Winter back to their wintery home when summer claimed the land of L'pilth.

Obstacles continued to test them, from the land to bandits.

As if someone intentionally placed every possible trouble before them.

Each guard pair worked together to deal with threats, those older teaching the younger ones their skills.

Her weapon vibrated against her side, making her pull it from its loop.

A warning undead approached.

The distant low told her what form it would take.

"Corpse hunter," she called out.

"Good ear," one of the older guards replied, "What else?"

"There could be one being silent while the other is giving the cry," she replied, scanning the landscape.

"When did you learn that?" Fab asked, pacing beside the Queen's conveyance, his spells lowering the already arctic air to colder temperatures.

"Vigil of Grella Harth," Siolobha scowled, then pulled the chime as the caravan halted, preparing for battle.

Setting the chime on the ground, she felt for vibrations, trying to filter out those of her allies.

She practiced with the guards who could hear through the ground so she had some of their tricks.

Two faint vibrations.

No, that wasn't right.

"Three approaching," a guard lifted his head from the ground, "One that direction, two there."

Siolobha frowned at the last one coming from a third direction, "What of the fourth?"

"There is no fourth."

She pulled up the chime, put it away, wondering how to practice it better.

Her war pick at the ready, she prepared for a fight.

The first appeared, followed by the second and third as expected.

She wasn't near the fights, so she kept watching around in case something else attacked.

Which is why she reacted before the other guards.

Her pick slammed into the head of the creature as she twisted to clear the suddenly frozen solid body.

It hit the ground, rolling as pieces splintered off of it, until it came to stop.

Then it crumbled into a pile.

She scanned the land around them, alert for more enemies.

Only silence greeted them.

"May I look over that chime?" Fab asked politely.

Siolobha handed it over, continuing her guard.

"The chime's spell is changing."

Siolobha frowned, "How?"

"There is a sentience to this item. It's changing such it aids you better," Fab handed the chime back with utmost care, "Was this a gift from the one who gave you the war pick?"

"Yes," she gently put the chime back.

Sentient magic items were worth more than the most powerful magic item without sentience.

They acted like partners, sometimes shifting their abilities to better suit who held them, evolving over time to become formidable powers.

Z'ronia let go of this item. No, she said the item would serve better in Siolobha's hands than hers.

She looked at her war pick, then Fab.

He nodded at her silent question, before moving back to the queen.

"Thank you," she whispered to both her war pick and the chime.

A slight vibration came from both, a sure sign both acknowledged her appreciation.

The caravan began again, moving towards their goal.

Even if it was glacial slow progress.

Z'ronia stood vigil for a village healer.

The woman died in her sleep after a long battle with a wasting disease.

However, she supplied a cure for that same disease before exhaling her last breath.

Z'ronia heard about her passing from the village one over after destroying a thief and his posse in one of their hides.

The entire village stood vigil for the healer, even children who could barely hold a weapon.

It spoke to how much impact the healer had on the village.

Familiar wingbeats made Z'ronia turn her head towards the sky.

Rathi's voice spoke gently to the villagers, commiserating the death of the healer, before speaking of the healer's triumphs in life.

Z'ronia wondered at the bonds Rathi formed with her people.

More than how Grella formed hers, Rathi united diverse people from many different backgrounds.

Z'ronia knew a rogue stood nearby, the nearly undetectable tang of a familiar poison with the old forge bite of a fire-edged shiv.

The combination meant the rogue once belonged to the Order of Smiles. Thus named for how they smiled so normally before killing their opponents.

Grella found a poem that seemed to indicate at one point the Order of Smiles had been led by a lich who only took jobs which helped their community become stronger. It had been a point of hope for Z'ronia once that there were liches like herself out there, at least until so many run ins with the worst left her feeling alone in the whole world.

Except she wasn't anymore.

Rathi's scent drew her out of her reverie.

"I am grateful you arrived first," Rathi's tone full of appreciation.

Z'ronia bowed her head slightly.

"Any issues during the day?"

"I outed and removed the thieves from their hide. They had a strange item with them which prevented the warning spell to sound," Z'ronia answered.

"You mean the awful noise before an attack?"

Z'ronia turned her head, identifying the speaker as a child, "Do you have some magic of the elements?"

Rathi knelt, her tone warming, "You make lightning, right?"

A crackle sounded then fizzled, "I'm not good yet."

"When the awful noise sounds, it is from the spell warning intruders are coming. However, it could be at some distance," Z'ronia explained.

"Why do I hear it, but no one else?"

At Rathi's touch, Z'ronia knelt, "The spell warns those who are elementalists. Those who can summon lightning, fire, rain or crack the earth. If you listen closely, you can tell where the warning is coming from and how close to you it is. In time you may be able to call the land to your aid."

"Like when the wind hugs me?"

"Hugs?" Z'ronia wasn't familiar with a spell like that.

A new voice chimed in, "When he's scared, he forms a wind shield. Well crafted for one so young."

Z'ronia nodded, "Exactly like when the wind hugs you. The land is responding to your need, strengthening it. Though you need to be cautious. Some spells become very different since the land loves elementalists greatly."

"Like what?"

The spell sounded an alarm.

She stood facing the direction they approached from.

"I believe an unchanged spell would highlight it," Rathi's smile sounded in her voice, "Perhaps the one you used against mounted enemies?"

The spell required someone to direct her to the enemy, like Grella did during some of the wars.

Many bards assumed it was a dual cast spell, one where two casters combine their disparate powers into one balanced spell. In a roundabout way it was a dual cast, just a caster and one to target it to an enemy.

The trick to this spell was how many Z'ronia would catch in the area without harming her allies.

Except with the land helping, she wasn't sure of its capabilities.

"How many?" Z'ronia asked Rathi.

"As many as I am," Rathi split into separate parts, wingbeats lifting the vampire into the air.

Focusing ahead, she readied the spell.

She'd only done this with one person yelling.

How many she could really do hadn't been tested.

Rumbles echoed off the cliff walls, the sound of a few dozen horses galloping as one herd.

"Make sure to keep watch behind," Z'ronia stated, "This could be a pincher attack."

Air changed at the entrance to the canyons as the hoofbeats started to lose their echoes from the walls.

Rathi's voice called from multiple directions.

Z'ronia snapped the spell word focusing on where the voices would converge.

The ground shuddered then she felt heat and swirling air, followed by the smell of lava. Screams reached her, then cut short

The spell would split the earth beneath the target enough to drop them into a pit.

"Lava pits with a tornado keeping them inside until they are covered in lava," Rathi reformed beside Z'ronia, "Our land is particularly angry with intruders based on how it likes your offensive spells."

Z'ronia shook her head, "It likes all spells. The reinforcement spells I apply to rebuild are made stronger with the land's aid."

"Is that why Kelir has doors which withstand rams?" Rathi hummed, "How often can you cast those spells?"

"Twice per day without impacting my ability to meet enemies. Five per day if I don't need to fight."

"Is that why you take a little while to return to the keep after an incursion?"

Z'ronia smiled, "Partly. I also pick up shipments so the villagers can continue working in their village, or can visit others more often without the need to be carrying goods."

"How much of a shipment could you carry? I have some thoughts on goods we bring in across the boundary."

The child touched Z'ronia's hip, "Will I be able to do spells like that?"

"In time," Z'ronia knelt, "I can teach you four spells which form the basis of more complex ones."

Others crowded around Z'ronia as she taught simple spells to the children, and a few of the elders who'd never seen them before.

Z'ronia halted as she felt the Grasp reaching out beneath the ground.

It gripped the soul then whisked away.

"To the ground from all came, she has returned. May we all find such a cycle peacefully when our time comes," Z'ronia intoned gently.

Rathi and other voices called L'pilth's vigil ending, "To our tie to the land and those who have gone before, the cycle continues."

The villagers broke apart, going back to their day.

Z'ronia walked to Plodder who pawed the ground.

She pulled an apple from a bag, held it for him to eat.

"I've been meaning to ask about the green apples. Do they have seeds?"

Z'ronia shrugged, pulled another apple, "I don't know. I only feed them to my mounts. They enjoy them."

After a few moments, Rathi sighed, "Few seeds. Very tiny compared to the red variety."

"Even the smallest seeds may grow strong," Z'ronia pulled a pouch from her saddle bags, "It would take me some time to resupply this powder, however it will make those seeds flourish."

Rathi's fingers touched her metal covered ones, conveying warmth, "Perhaps my arborists will return the favor by supplying you with a few of our red ones so you have variety."

Plodder neighed, then Z'ronia heard an oomph from Rathi as metal thudded with flesh.

Z'ronia held her laughter back, "I believe you have made Plodder very happy with that future."

"I fear what happens if Plodder is angry," Rathi gripped Z'ronia's shoulder, "Daylight comes. I need to retreat."

"I will stand guard, King Rathi," Z'ronia patted Plodder. They parted ways, to their respective duties.

Chapter 21

Slashed Heart

"Then when our time comes tolling"

Rathi bade farewell to the Spring court, the promise of sound games to be made available on their next visit.

Z'ronia had departed earlier to deal with an incursion at the far end of L'pilth.

With nightfall, Rathi could take up her part of the patrol.

Splitting into her flock, she took to the air.

Swooping through the spires and canyons, she scanned for anything her people needed to be happy or defend them against.

An hour passed easily.

Then the smell of blood drew her entire flock to a village near Darksteel Keep.

Hoping they had to slaughter several of their animals, she dove down then under an overhang.

Bodies.

Rage filled her as she assumed her normal form, drawing her weapon.

This village had taken her a century of effort to bring to L'pilth.

As she walked, counting the bodies of elders, children and adults, she felt all that effort wasted.

Satyrs were magical people.

The beer, wine and ales made here sold for a hundred times the cost to get them through to the Boundary.

This clan had been the best of the best at their craft.

To see such devastation so close to the heart of her kingdom, and to one people she swore to protect and nourish.

Hatred burned through her as she came to the final home.

The Great Elder's residence offered respite from hard work, becoming the village's meeting hall.

Instead bodies were strung up on the pillars and walls.

A tapestry hung in front of the Great Elder's body, hiding all but the dripping viscera. Words read clear through the blood.

"No knight nor vampire can protect from us."

Rathi roared her outrage.

She fought the intense desire to carve a bloody path into the kingdoms beneath hers. To etch her vengeance upon their people for each crime they visited on her charges.

Yet if she left, her living people would be in danger.

Horrifying images of spells empowered by the satyrs tortured her will, mocking her competing duties.

Duties to send the dead to the other side peacefully against the duties to the living from threats.

Trembling she blinked back tears.

She knew everyone in this village.

Young, old, hale and sick.

Jerking she realized one wasn't accounted for.

The child of revelry, Diona, who would make a drink to change all drinks. So said the Great Elder with fondness months ago.

Standing, she vowed to get the child back, or to ensure she wasn't used in a necromantic spell.

A noise made her whirl, blade swinging out.

Only for Z'ronia's sledge hammer to arrest the slice.

"King Rathi?"

Rathi exhaled, withdrew her blade, "Black Knight. This…"

She had no words.

A newborn cry roused her to a defensive position.

Only to realize Z'ronia cradled the infant against her armor.

A satyr.

"I'll attend to the dead. You need to attend to the living," Z'ronia lowered her hammer, offered the child.

Rathi sheathed her weapon, took the baby with both hands, curling over the infant, tears falling.

"They know I can't leave my kingdom, nor launch an attack for this atrocity," Rathi shivered, "They took this precious village from me to prove they can and will again."

Z'ronia's gauntlet gripped her shoulder, the comfort immediate, "Attend to your duties, King Rathi. I will handle this."

In the deep voice rang a promise.

We'll get them for this.

Rathi inhaled, exhaled, "I'll send some of my guards out to collect their artifacts. At least their culture will continue."

Rathi walked out, plotting how to take the price of crossing her from the heathen kingdoms south of her lands.

Z'ronia knew what Rathi did to woo the satyrs to her rule.

How Rathi delighted in each new drink, each new decoration from the village. Took refuge in this village when the trials of leadership weighed on her. Held each newborn with reverence and delight as she met her new charge for the first time.

The cut to her heart gouged deep.

There was only one answer for such provocation: prove those who'd done this were not safe.

Kneeling in the midst of death, Z'ronia called on the spells to track casters.

She laid counters to these spells on each one she cast, but others were not so meticulous.

These butchers, in arrogance or ignorance, left their spirit essence in their spells.

Drawing those essences into a tracking spell, Z'ronia knew the direction they fled, and they had crossed the Boundary a long time ago.

As she knew where they retreated, she knew what else the enemy stole more than their lives.

They took the spirits of the dead.

Z'ronia urged the earth to claim the bodies deep into the ground.

Then she stalked out.

Plodder huffed, drawing her to his side.

"Go back to the keep, Plodder. I need to make this trip solo."

He butted her shoulder, snorted.

"It is a long distance through the untamed earth paths. I can travel them easier alone. I need speed in this hunt."

Plodder rattled his barding.

Laying a hand on his head she whispered, "Guard Rathi and the keep. I will slam a blow so devastating to the enemy they will hesitate to engage us again for a few months."

Plodder snorted into her helm, then turned and trotted away.

Z'ronia slipped into the earth paths.

Since she discovered the first leading beyond Laeb, she'd taken an hour each day to travel others.

She knew the thieves ran to Sla'der.

Moving down the path, she readied her weapons, physical and magical.

No one harmed anyone in her care and left unscathed.

Constantly checking the direction of her prey, she strode through the earth, hearing burrowing creatures around her.

Her prey halted somewhere ahead.

A respite?

A trap?

As she closed the gap between them, she heard wagon wheels, tramping feet, voices calling and answering.

Sounds fitting a large city.

She hated cities.

Too noisy for her to detect threats.

However, if she struck quickly, she may be able to take down the enemy before they could summon help, or escape into the crowds.

The earth paths under the city were chaotic, twisted by the buildings erected above. She backtracked and wove through, seeking to get closer and closer to where her enemies stayed.

Voices lessened above her, quieting, individual voices no longer muddled by crowds.

"Cry, goat legs," a nasty voice laughed.

The voice who answered made Z'ronia tense, "Please, let me go! I've done nothing."

Diona, the name shot from Rathi's memories into Z'ronia's thoughts.

Another survivor of the village to protect.

A yelp launched Z'ronia upward, weapons held in hand.

Chapter 22

Retaliation

"We join joyously with the Grasp"

Diona scrambled back from the men who'd slaughtered her people, only to jerk to a stop as the leash tied to her torso snapped taut, her bound hands useless.

"You are a prime component for a spell. We'll get top furs for you," the largest man pulled on the leash, hauling her back to their table.

They sat outside an inn, indulging in a meal as passersby scoffed at her.

Sobbing, she scrambled with her hooves against the smooth street, struggling to get free.

The air stilled a moment, then fog erupted from the ground, instantly blocking all sight.

"Spell!" The smallest man snapped.

The leash loosened as she heard muffled sounds like chairs scrapping on stone.

Silence made the next sound echo eerily.

Metal on stone.

Clack. Clack. Clack. Clack.

She scrunched down as she realized the sound was footsteps on the street.

Was this the one purchasing her?

Then the fog parted, light from lanterns bathing the figure approaching with golden hues.

Black armor, two weapons held at ready, a dark aura spreading out. The new knight of her king.

She screamed in hope, "Black Knight!"

"You should have stayed in L'pilth, Black Knight," the large man laughed, hefting a two-handed axe, "We don't leave race traitors alive."

The deep voice spoke with dark intent, "I will not allow enemies to escape my reach."

The smallest man snapped a word, purple bolts lancing at the Black Knight.

Stones rose in the air, crumbling under the onslaught, filling the air with dust.

Diona squeaked as she was lifted, the leather leash pulling taut.

Only to find herself face to helm with the Black Knight.

"You destroyed a village of L'pilth," the Black Knight's voice echoed down the streets, "For that dishonor, you all pay!"

No word, no gesture preceded the fire from the lanterns bursting their cages, rising over Diona and the Black Knight.

Then the flame crashed down into the streets, scorching bodies to ashes.

Not the whole body, Diona noticed as the flames rushed into the city.

Flames left the heads as if a sword slashed through the neck on each person, separating them from the destruction below them.

"Break your bonds and return to the other side!" The Black Knight's voice chased the flames.

Diona felt the magic in the words, the touch of the Grasp terrifying her as she clutched the Black Knight.

"Goodbye, child of revelry," the Great Elder's voice made her look up.

The crystal vials the men had carried in bandoliers lay shattered on the ground. The vials they'd fed the spirits of her family into when they cast their horrible spell.

She looked up at the Black Knight, "What did you do?"

"I killed every person in this city."

"No, the second spell."

"Any undead save for a lich would be forced to the other side and the Grasp's care."

She looked at the vials, then hugged the Black Knight, crying.

The knight knelt, shifted her only slightly.

Wiping an eye clear, she watched the Black Knight collect the heads of the men who'd taken her.

"What are you going to do with their heads?" She hiccuped.

"I will present them to King Rathi as proof they will not attack us again," the Black Knight shoved the heads into a sack, tied it closed, then stood, "Close your eyes, Diona."

"You know my name?" She looked at the knight, then closed her eyes, burrowing her face against the armor, "Why do I need to close my eyes."

"I know your name from King Rathi. It is easier on you for this next spell if you close your eyes. Are they closed?"

"Yes, Black Knight," Diona gripped her savior tighter, "Are we going home?"

"To L'pilth," the Black Knight replied before the world seemed to spin, even with her eyes closed.

Diona placed a hand over her eyes, "Thank you."

"For what?" The Black Knight asked.

She could feel the Black Knight walking as she answered, "For coming for me."

"That is my duty and honor, Diona," the Black Knight stated softly, "I defend when the enemy is around, I avenge when they flee."

Grief welled up inside her, "My mama and papa?"

"Their spirits are with the Grasp as their mortal remains are buried. They are safe from our enemies."

"Mama, papa," Diona sobbed, clutching the only solid thing in her world: the firm armor of the Black Knight.

Ghir'ali paced the entrance hall, the guards who'd gone out to help the Black Knight long retired to their beds.

She...he left before the minotaurs arrived, the bodies missing.

They'd have to stand vigil for them and needed to know where to do so.

A faint scent of freshly turned earth warned him the Black Knight approached.

Between one blink and the next, the Black Knight stood where there'd been only air.

Inhaling to berate the lich, he halted.

A satyr child lay in the lich's arms, shaking.

"Diona, you can look now," the soft tone made Ghir'ali wait.

The child peeked out, her face a mess from dried and new tears, eyes red and her breaths hiccuping every other breath.

"Let's get to Hagh," Ghir'ali huffed a breath, "Rathi went out after he brought the baby here."

A breeze swept by them, "I let Rathi know I've returned."

Clopping deeper into the keep, Ghir'ali asked, "Where did you go?"

"If my sense of direction is correct, the city of Mol'dra."

Ghir'ali stopped, "Repeat that."

The Black Knight paused turned, but the child snapped, "He came for me in Mol'dra. The awful men were gonna sell me as a spell component."

The mulish look on the child's face made him adjust his next words, "That is several weeks travel for us, a couple days for Rathi. How?"

"The enemy used a portal node. I passed it on my hunt," said the Black Knight.

"I mean how did you get after them so fast?" Ghir'ali felt the daggers the child glared at him.

"I have ways that take patience to learn, but can enable me to travel quickly alone. If you want, I can take you on a short jaunt like I do Plodder so you can understand better," the Black Knight continued walking.

Ghir'ali caught up to him, "We'd never be able to get to her in time."

"If our enemies take my retaliation for the warning I meant it to be, we won't need to get to their kingdom in time, only to where they attack us here."

Chapter 23

Comfort

"On the other side"

Rathi flung herself into the keep, the words from Z'ronia lashing her to greater speed.

"I have recovered Diona. She needs to see her king. We are going to Master Healer Hagh."

Rushing to the healer's domain, Rathi caught herself on the doorway.

Sitting on the bed, Z'ronia held Diona, who sniffled as Hagh cleaned wounds on her wrists.

Diona hugged one of Z'ronia's arms, pressed into the armor as if the lich stood as keep walls.

Z'ronia turned her head, bowed her head, "King Rathi."

Rathi eased inside, moved to the shivering satyr girl, "Diona."

The satyr launched herself at Rathi.

Rathi caught the child as she wound her arms around her neck.

The sobs nearly broke Rathi in two.

Rubbing Diona up and down her back, Rathi's eyes rose to Z'ronia's helm.

"Will they come again?"

Z'ronia lifted a bag from the floor, held it out, "Their heads as part of the price for their incursion. I killed the residents of Mol'dra as additional incentive to not attack again."

Rathi knew Z'ronia guarded her back as well as carrying out her desire.

Decimating the capital city of Sla'der would send a warning through all the kingdoms: come for L'pilth's citizens and you face the Black Knight at your seat of power.

Rathi would guard the land while her knight rode out to deal justice.

Taking the bag, she spoke with appreciation, "Thank you."

"I will go see about Plodder. The infant could also use some time with our king."

Z'ronia vanished.

Ghir'ali stepped forward, "I'll see the tribute to your rooms, my king."

Rathi hesitated to hand it over, knowing the precious gift Z'ronia brought her.

It wasn't the love spoken of in bard poems, with oaths being exchanged to be true to one another until death.

Instead, there stood the promise of being the crushing weapon against their enemies while also protecting those Rathi held dear, even if Z'ronia had to ride to the ends of the world to do so. A devotion to Rathi in all her selves, from king, friend and to something which could be if they wanted it to be.

Worth more than anything she'd been given before, Rathi knew she'd never dishonor the gesture.

Looking at Ghir'ali, she saw his acceptance, "As you wish, my king."

Hugging the child returned to her, Rathi knew she would stand side by side with Z'ronia. Until the end of time and unto their passage to the other side.

Z'ronia dealt with several more intrusions on L'pilth, most with more force than needed, but she wanted it clear she would not suffer another assault on her people by the savage kingdoms south of her kingdom.

It felt familiar and different.

Like when she rode with Grella, yet more.

Pangs of grief followed her inside the keep, the warmth of midday on her armor losing to the chill inside.

Ghir'ali's distinctive breathing announced his arrival.

"Rathi needs you," he stated before exiting, "He is in his rooms. I'll see to Plodder."

Worried, Z'ronia used the earth path to outside Rathi's rooms.

She knocked, "King Rathi?"

Rustle of cloth over cloth, a sniffle, "Come in."

Z'ronia opened the door, stepped inside before closing the door.

She smelled tears and faint blood.

"What troubles you, King Rathi?" Z'ronia did not want Rathi to be sad.

"Grief," the voice thickened with sadness, "I lose to either those kingdoms, or to the Grasp."

Z'ronia knew Rathi's heartaches from a thousand dead vassals, lovers, friends and advisors as if it was her own.

She felt it as keenly as Rathi when she lost a dear companion.

"I understand," Z'ronia simply replied.

"I know in the vampire court I was brought into there was lasting friendships and lovers, so grief wasn't something they experienced much. Since I left them, I am surrounded by the Grasp's work constantly."

Z'ronia moved over to the bed where Rathi's voice emanated from, sat, "Time moves differently when you are alone or in the midst of immortals than when you work with mortals. You appreciate the time more with them since they leave so soon."

"I wouldn't give up these friendships and loves for the world. They keep me whole even when their death tears me to pieces."

Z'ronia reached out her hand, rested it gently on Rathi's, "Sometimes, we also need the stability of immortals. You know this well."

Rathi's hand turned over and her fingers gripped Z'ronia's, "No matter how many lovers I lost, the sidhe are more important as friends than choosing one of them for love."

"Just as the friendships of Grella's company was worth more than the efforts needed to be human for them. Each is a part of me and their loss to the Grasp like someone sliced slivers off my spirit each time it happened. I would never want to be back in the cave after having those friendships."

An arm wrapped around her as a body pressed against her armor, "I miss them so much already."

Z'ronia nodded, "We will always miss them, yet they will not be forgotten while we live."

Rathi shook, her breaths gasping out, "It hurts."

Z'ronia held Rathi, lowering her voice, "It does."

Holding one another, they grieved their lost family and friends.

Chapter 24

Preparation

"[Chorus] Dance with the Grasp"

Siolobha took her shift with the Queen of Winter.

They made it to their winter home during this time of year, only to find the Queen rapidly weakening, even in the height of their season.

The other courts were called, two arriving within a week, the other still distant as they returned from L'pilth.

Vigil approached with the promise of trouble.

The Queen's consort leaned in briefly, then bowed his head at her soft words.

He left.

"Siolobha," the Queen gestured, "Come."

She stepped over to the ailing queen, "My queen?"

The queen gripped Siolobha's wrist, the warmth alarming against her skin, "Cold fire."

"I'll have them brought," at the queen's head shake she asked, "Cold fire?"

She rasped, "Allies turn the tide. Cold fire against demon flame."

"Our allies are gathering, my queen. We'll have plenty of cold fires to help our people withstand vigil."

"The summoning...the summoning sooner...don't wait...purple rain," the Queen closed her eyes and fell into a sleep.

Gently, Siolobha set the queen's hand back beside her, before returning to her post.

Fab entered carrying a snow blanket with him, the Queen's consort returning to her side.

"Something wrong?" Fab asked, unfurling the blanket before laying it over the Queen with a whispered spell word.

The temperature in the room dropped.

"She said Allies turn the tide. Cold fire against demon flame. Summoning sooner. Don't wait. Purple rain?" Siolobha frowned, "I don't understand what she meant."

"Demons? I'll speak with the King. Perhaps we need to summon Rathi along with our distant sibling court sooner. We can also send a call to the Tower of Floods to aid us."

Siolobha considered the sleeping Queen.

What had the Queen seen that they needed to prepare for?

She carried the stone to summon Z'ronia, wondering when she should cast the stone into a fire.

Perhaps the Queen meant to look for purple rain to start, or purple rain was too late to summon Z'ronia?

Fab and the Queen's consort made changes so the Queen's final hours would pass peacefully.

Only the Queen hissed out a breath and drew no new one.

They stood still, waiting for her to inhale.

Only she did not, her skin changing to warmer hues.

Fab looked at Siolobha, "I'll inform the King. Please begin preparing her for vigil."

As he left, Siolobha felt the chime in her pouch ring once, as if to say something dreadful raced their way.

Rathi gathered her weapons and armor.

The Winter Court called for aid in vigil.

Ghir'ali fretted, "The Black Knight should be told of this."

"I cannot wait. Tell him when he returns to the keep that I've been summoned. He'll understand," she paused, frowned, "He may be requested as well. One of the Winter Court, their new guard has a stone to reach the Black Knight if needed."

"What of us?"

"Ring the bell for everyone to go to ground. The Black Knight has reinforced all the villages so they have better protections."

"If they attack the keep, we have no way to repel them. It will be a siege, though we can last a while with our supplies," Ghir'ali argued.

Vorbe's voice interrupted, "There is one way to drive them back."

"What do you mean?" Rathi shouldered her gear.

"Come on down to your deepest room. The Black Knight found it yesterday, then had to fend off incursions since," the old bard moved with a shake of his head, "You'd think destroying a capital city would make them halt until they could contain him."

They arrived at the room, one Rathi recalled briefly exploring when she first arose to power.

The altar in the middle gave her a creepy sensation when she drew too close.

Her mages at the time said the altar was tied with death.

Vorbe nodded to the altar, "The Black Knight said it has death and elemental magic bound into it. It also has bardic magic."

"You know what this does?" Rathi demanded.

"Impolin had one like it, but it was arcane magic crossed with death and bardic," he smiled sadly, "If the capital was in danger, a bard or angelic mage could power up the altar to unleash an attack which ignores citizens of the realm. It was said it could inundate the capital in an instant, destroying even undead and demons with its magic. The cost was the life of whoever powered it up."

Rathi touched Vorbe's shoulder, "I am not..."

"I know you would never ask," Vorbe turned and faced Rathi, "But I know what I would do if it came down to one life against many. You said the Black Knight could be called. Your enemies may be waiting for this moment to attack, when both of our mightiest defenders are elsewhere."

Rathi looked away, then at Vorbe, already hurting with what could happen before she could return, "Only if there is no other way."

"Just promise me one thing," Vorbe smiled, "Make my song known."

Rathi nodded gravely, then turned to Ghir'ali, "Tell everyone to secure themselves now. The Black Knight will hear it and understand my command."

"What if you don't return?" Ghir'ali asked.

Rathi considered her heart, then ordered, "The Black Knight is your ruler, should he remain."

"My king," Ghir'ali hesitated, "Please come back."

Rathi looked at Vorbe then her seneschal, "I will do what I am able. I cannot promise more. Just as you cannot promise to be here should the other kingdoms invade, only do what you can to hold them back."

At their grim expressions, she indicated she was ready to get to vigil.

The world faded around her before flaring back.

Instead she stood in a wintery land.

Following one of the sidhe to the King of Winter, she regretted not being able to tell Z'ronia she had left and she was her successor should she fall.

As well as saying the three words circling her heart since Z'ronia held her as they both grieved their lost ones.

Chapter 25

War

"[Chorus] Until you return alive"

Z'ronia heard the drums signaling all of Rathi's vassals to get to shelter.

Shortly before it sounded, she'd dispatched a raiding party, sending their spirits to the Grasp as the sentinel spell signaled more invaders.

She turned to the village she just defended and boomed, "Get to the hall and bar the doors!"

Plodder tromped over to her, bumping her with his head.

"Rathi is calling for all his people to shelter," she whispered to Plodder, "Something must be coming behind these skirmishers."

She took them both through the earth paths to the next attack, dispatching them as fast as she could.

Riding up on the last of the current warnings, she heard soft voices.

"The master is securing the frost corpse. We need to get deep enough in she can break through easily," one tittered.

"Don't see why we need the sidhe to be brought over," another groused.

Plodder turned the corner, just as the Grasp brush her.

She knew then the voices didn't belong to mortals.

Liches.

"Well, well. Here is the Black Knight and...you have to be joking!" The titterer snarled, "A lich."

Dismounting, she told Plodder, "Move back."

She drew her weapons, enhancing her voice, "This is my land. Leave."

"Oh, a goody-jarred lich wants to challenge us? This will be fun," the titterer laughed, "I haven't had a good fight in ages."

A scrap beside her gave her enough warning.

Her mace slammed first into the body, the sledgehammer pulverizing it the next with snapping bones.

The Grasp seized the spirit, the lich's spirit screaming as it was pulled to the other side.

"He was young and had a lousy attitude," Titterer snickered.

Wind warned her, giving her enough time to dodge as magic roared by her.

She snapped one of the modified spells, then cursed as it was countered by her opponent.

It felt familiar and dangerous.

Hissing another spell, higher level, she was knocked off her feet as her spell fizzled.

She struck stone, her metal armor ringing with the impact.

"Older liches than you have fallen to me," Titterer began chanting.

A spell she knew would turn the area and the sixteen nearest villages into molten rock, even with her new improvements.

Z'ronia called to the land, pleading for its aid, unleashing one of her unmodified spells with a roar, seeking to stop the lich before he finished his spell.

Then she knew nothing.

She jerked into alertness, reaching for her weapons.

Only for the familiar bump of Plodder's head to halt the motion.

The Grasp no longer paced under the ground.

Siting up, she felt stones and sand fall off her, though the sound echoed through her armor oddly.

"Plodder?" Her voice sounded soft and muffled.

Another bump.

Clutching him, she shivered.

Whispering a spell to determine what magic remnants lingered, she read the results.

She called on wind to crush the lich like she'd done to the flyers. This time instead of swatting her opponents from the sky, a massive lightning bolt struck the ground, centered on the lich.

She'd been in the blast radius.

Ringing began in her ears.

She knew what that meant.

Casting a healing spell on herself, she breathed a sigh of relief as her hearing returned and the various aches in her bones subsided.

Then she cursed.

She couldn't do too many more massive spells, even with the land helping.

Hoping she'd ended the last threat, she mounted, "Slow ride towards the keep, Plodder."

His snort was a welcomed sound.

Siolobha stood at the entrance to the healers' cave, braced for another wave.

Skeletons, carcasses, corpse hunters, and flying creatures like those at Grella's vigil came on the sidhe as waves from the ocean.

Rathi darted across the field, taking out entire lines as the sidhe of all courts waged battle.

The Queen's corpse lay in the center of their defenses, the King of Winter just a little ways away.

Her war pick instantly froze the corpse hunter attempting to get pass her and into the wounded healers frantically rushed back into the battle. She kicked the corpse hunter, shattering the remains.

So many more ran towards her.

Fab's voice boomed across the field.

Swords glittered into existence, began swinging at enemies, the enchanted weapons made inroads on the undead as if a fifth court also in the height of its season joined them.

Then the clouds above turned greenish in color.

Rain began falling.

Purple rain.

Fab's scream drew her gaze to him.

His robe began dissolving as he fought to maintain the spell. Several guards nearby lifted up shields to protect him, only for their shields to begin melting.

Siolobha looked at the purple rain, then pulled the stone out of her pouch.

She tossed it into the cold fire, praying she summoned Z'ronia in time.

Then she caught sight of a terrible new force cresting the distant hill.

Glittering gems seemed to grin with malice from skulls.

Liches.

One gestured to Fab, firing off a spell with a horrid laugh.

Only Rathi intercepted it, taking the blow to his leg, bisecting an undead approaching Fab with his sword.

Fab roared another spell, tearing off his robes, holes simultaneously crossing his body from the acid.

Wind roared by, flowing upward against the rain, carrying it out over the undead army.

"What is this?"

Siolobha glanced back at the healer, then the brazier with the stone, "An ally who promised to help with a vigil gave that to me. She said to put it in fire to call her."

"It's glowing orange."

Flicking a glance at the stone, she agreed.

The glyphs flared orange in the midst of cold blue flame, as if both summer and winter co-existed in the same space without destroying each other.

"She didn't say what it would look like," Siolobha wanted to kick herself as she recalled Z'ronia couldn't see.

"How soon will she arrive?"

"I don't know," Siolobha gritted her teeth, wanting to attack, but held back.

Z'ronia would have a better chance against the liches than her.

Like should fight like, or their equal.

Then the undead stormed the healers' cave, forcing Siolobha to fight with all she had.

Her arms vibrated with her blows, her weapons whirling to strike skeletons, carcasses and other monstrosities.

Panting, she struggled to hold them back, keeping them from the wounded.

Then one knocked her down, planted a foot on her chest, pinning her to the ground.

Fear filled her as another raised a two-handed axe overhead, paused a moment.

Then descended.

Chapter 26

Choice

"[Chorus] Unless in undeath"

Z'ronia rushed down the earth paths, following the clinking of the stone she'd given Siolobha.

She'd dropped off Plodder at Darksteel Keep then run down the paths towards the distant sidhe.

Once she exited L'pilth the paths, she choose those paths she ran smooth over the months.

Only once she reached the end of those, the paths roughened, slowing her down.

Cursing those who'd never used the same spell, working on those path like her, Z'ronia trudged on, passing villages, towns and cities.

A pang of nostalgia struck her as she entered paths she knew.

Yereen.

A kingdom she no longer called home, yet the earth held the same well-trod roads she'd laid down over the decades she served as a knight.

Refocusing on the sound, she exited Yereen, traveling south as fast as she could.

With relief, the sound grew softer, meaning she grew closer to it.

She felt the fire the stone sat in, arrowing on it for her arrival.

"Siolobha!"

The voice shouted as if in warning.

Z'ronia burst out of the earth, using the shout to direct her into the fight, she swung out with her sledgehammer.

Bones snapped, blowing the enemy back away from her.

"Z'ronia, there!" Siolobha cried out.

Z'ronia flung out a spell, wind lashing out at the target Siolobha shouted at.

"There are liches," Siolobha stated in a softer voice, her words indicating she rose from the ground.

Commanding the wind to form a web around her, Z'ronia sought the liches' location.

Only for her magic to meet ice and death.

She never had met someone with such powerful magic.

"No," Siolobha gasped, "They took our queen."

The Queen of Winter, risen as an undead with powers Z'ronia knew she couldn't counter.

The mere rising of the Queen shredded magic all around, binding the elements to her will.

Z'ronia knew the entire battlefield stilled as vibrations halted.

Except she could feel something approaching at a distance, like a hint of thunder rolling closer.

"Siolobha," Z'ronia braced for her last spell, "Another army approaches. I will deal with the Queen and the undead, but if the second army is not of those groups, you will need to be ready to defend."

"Z'ronia, what do you mean?"

Z'ronia turned her head to the sidhe she would have loved to be friends with, "There is only one spell which can claim the Queen before her power enables her to break the bonds the liches tried to weave around her," Z'ronia turned back to the swirling nexus growing stronger, her magics flaring as the Queen's aura brushed her, "I hope I will not see you on the other side for some time."

Z'ronia bellowed the spell which would end all undead, even the caster.

Agony burst in the center of her being, metal exploding inside her chest.

Her last thought chased her down: Her soul jar broke inside her.

Xyan felt their approach through the slumbering trees.

Something unnatural with evil intent neared her home.

Standing from feeding her pets, their wings fluttering with their delight in the meat, she cast out her magic.

Demonic mages marched beside carcasses, corpse hunters, skeletons, and a demon.

A full demon unlike the demonic mages strode with malice in her woods.

Calling her minions to bar doors and take up positions to defend the deity's body, she pulled her staves from their leather loops.

Only the demon army marched on by.

Confused, she whispered a command to her Eclipse Hawks to stand ready.

Whoever the demons marched on may not withstand the attack.

Meaning the army may turn and attack her next.

Magic swirled in the distance, bringing the unmistakable feel of winter sidhe magic. Only it was infected with death.

Xyan turned to mount one of her hawks, knowing something terrible must have happened to the Winter Court for their magic to take on death magic.

Only for everything to go white.

Her hands lay empty of her weapons.

Whirling, she sought who to attack.

"Youngling," a voice she dearly missed preceded her mentor and partner appearing from the blankness, the whiteness parting like fog from sunlight.

"Dorrick! You took too long to get back," she chided, angry with him.

He pulled off his helm, then replied, "I am not back."

The sorrowful tone held her from hugging him, "What do you mean?"

"I died my final death, youngling," Dorrick held his helm under an arm, "You just saw who shattered me into a thousand tiny pieces."

"The demon," She growled, then flinched, "If you are here, does that mean I met my final end?"

"No. A lich cast the same ceremonial spell I told you went wrong a few millenniums ago, taking over half of our community with it. You were close enough to be caught in the range of it."

A shiver ran down her bones, "Does the caster have the strength to bring me back? The body hasn't rotted away yet and its undefended now."

He placed a hand on her chest, directly under her chin. Over where her soul jar rested with the best protections possible.

"Grasp is with her now. However, she will be alone on the field with that demon, save for a vampire. That demon will require many to bring her down and end her machinations."

She remembered he once said the tomb guardians left their charges thrice before, all to end a far greater threat to the world than a few thieves gaining powers they shouldn't have.

"This female demon is worthy of all tomb guardians charging her?"

His voice saddened as did his aura, "You were the only tomb guardian remaining in the world of the living. You have to decide if this is enough to warrant you charging alone."

"This other lich is not a Tomb Guardian? What style is she?"

"Born," Dorrick turned his head as if hearing something, "Make your decision, Xyan."

Gritting her teeth she snarled, "This demon will not continue while I have strength left. I charge!"

Dorrick nodded, stepping back, "Should you return to the living side, remember to send your call to arms far and wide. Your pets are akin to flocks nearby. You'll need them to last long enough in the battle ahead."

Others appeared around him, their vestments denoting they all were tomb guardians.

"Regardless of returning to the living side, or remaining here, you are part of our community. Remember that always," Dorrick inclined his head.

She jerked her head in an affirmative nod.

Chapter 27

Defenses

"[Chorus] Serve as Grasp's hands"

Rathi shivered, struggling against a familiar sensation stealing her strength. The same one only Z'ronia could cure.

Braced against Fab, they faced the undead.

Who halted before turning to where the Queen's body lay.

Only the body rose to its feet, the once kindly expression on the face replaced by the dull look of someone under suggestion.

Rathi bared her teeth, coiling to leap at the Queen.

Even if she was batted away, someone may be able to take the Queen down, bringing her true rest.

Only for the dear voice of Z'ronia to ring out with a spell full of determination and finality.

Rathi found herself standing in the middle of perfectly kept grounds, a single figure before her.

Lifting her hand, she found her weapon gone.

"No need for that, grandchild," the man smiled sadly, "You won't need to fight here."

"You are not my grandfather," Rathi snarled, recalling the faces of her grandparents from her past easily, "They died ages ago."

"I am not your birth family grandparent," he lifted his lips, the fangs clear to see, "I am the one who made your sire."

"The one he detested? The useless one?" Rathi scowled.

"Only useless to someone who has greed in their heart and spirit. To someone with honor and dignity, I am anything but that," the vampire swept a half kneel, "I am Chrather, Bloodelder of the Justices."

Justices.

The clan of vampires who rode out with only thoughts to good deeds and giving shelter to the weak.

Rathi shook her head, "I am not of that line."

Chrather straightened gracefully, "You are of my line, which means you are a member of the Justices. Come."

Rathi looked around, seeking a way back the battlefield, "I am needed elsewhere."

"You are on the other side, and anything back in the realm of the living has no hold over you for the time being."

"I have to stop the Queen!" Rathi gripped Chrather's arm, halting the vampire, "She has to be..."

"She is here, too," Chrather pointed with his chin.

Rathi looked, then dropped her hand.

The Queen stood among a group of Sidhe, a collection from all the four courts, looking relieved.

"The spell used by your love brought all undead on the battlefield here. Removing them from combat as surely as a scythe through rye fields."

"Z'ronia!" Rathi whirled, seeking her lich.

"She is not here. However, you need to make a decision."

Rathi turned back to Chrather, "What decision?"

"Would you return to the world of the living, if you could?"

There was some information hidden in the words.

Promising something that she'd never heard of.

Returning from the other side did not happen.

Then she knew an answer.

The only one she loved was here.

"I go where Z'ronia does," Rathi braced for a fight, "I will not lose her, not when I have just found her after so long alone."

Chrather smiled, "I await what her answer is. Let's go speak with the others here while hers is brought into the open."

"I will not accept anything but reunification," Rathi paced beside Chrather.

"The spell she used is very special. There is a chance to return, but her will deems the outcome. If she doesn't want to transverse the living world, you both would be welcomed here."

"What do you mean?"

"There are so many who die each day. Grasp alone would be overtaken without aid. We undead who have met our final end help. We are the Grasp's hands in all lands, securing those who have died and need to cross to this side. All undead," Chrather nodded to an approaching group, "Vampires, liches, ghosts, specters, wraiths, skeletons, carcasses, corpse hunters, and many other types. We who have free will help, or like the Queen, retire to bastions as guardians of the dead as they forget themselves until they can be reborn."

Something about the two liches amidst the group tickled Rathi's senses with familiarity. Yet she never met any good liches until Z'ronia.

Chrather greeted, "Rathi, may I present the parents of your love."

Rathi stared, too shocked to react initially.

Vorbe cursed as he hobbled with Octave's help.

After the Black Knight left Plodder, saying she needed to get to a vigil, enemies assaulted the walls of Darksteel Keep.

Within seconds the walls began crumbling, forcing Ghir'ali to order everyone deeper into the keep. One piece of the wall clipping Vorbe's ankle before he could get clear, slowing him down as the servants and healers rushed away faster than he could.

Only the defenders kept forfeiting more and more ground to the invaders as time passed.

Plodder trumpeted behind Vorbe, the clang of hooves on metal giving Vorbe a headache in conjunction with the clash of minotaur weapons against the enemy.

Octave stepped delicately as she braced him.

"Rathi won't have anything to come back to," Vorbe glanced back, winced as the mighty guards gave ground again, Plodder's legs giving them a moment to retreat to the next doorway.

They tried plugging the entrance but the fully armored enemies crushed or shoved the fallen out of their way.

He stopped, knowing there was only one solution.

Turning, he limped down a side corridor, leaving the group behind.

Octave nuzzled him before gripping him with her teeth, trying to stop him.

"I'm sorry," he patted her nose, "I have to go this way. I need to do this for them."

She took a step back, pulling him slightly back with her.

"I'm sorry," he petted her, "I have to save them. They need you. Your luck can spare a lot of harm. Go on Octave. Save them."

He could see her weighing him, then she let go.

She vanished, racing away.

Leaning on the wall for support, he forced himself onward.

He had to get to the altar before the enemies overran him.

Cursing under his breath at the pain stealing his strength, he pushed his body towards salvation.

The sounds of fighting faded slightly as he struggled ahead.

It felt like eternity before he turned the final corner to see the door to the altar room.

Not resting a moment, he limped faster, tears falling with each step.

Then he threw open the door, hugging the wood before shoving the door closed again.

Pulling down the bar, he panted.

Turning to face the altar, he bit his lip.

He shuffled towards it, pulling his bassoon out of its case.

He stumbled when the door behind him boomed under a blow.

Resisting his desire to look back, he gritted his teeth, taking those last steps with his remaining haste.

Leaning on the altar, he floundered.

He knew in Impolin, any song from a bard imbued with magic would trigger the altar.

Yet he couldn't think of a single song.

As if his mind was blank.

He fisted his hand on the altar, hit it, then growled, "Don't leave me yet. I need one song. Any song."

Thuds rained on the door behind him.

Like a drumbeat.

Inhaling, he put his lips to the bassoon and began playing, closing his eyes.

Behind his eyelids, the land of L'pilth lay below him, the view from the top of Darksteel Keep.

Only this view was different, the crags far shorter and less crowded.

A frayed-robed figure looked over the land, turning to a flamboyantly dressed person.

"I fear this enemy will launch another attack after this fight," the frayed-robe spoke gently with a roughened voice.

Flamboyant fingered a three-string instrument, the plink of fingers against the strings clear in the air, "The altar is complete. I will ensure if they attempt to run around you, they will not gain victory."

"I hoped another elementalist would be ready when they marched on us," frayed-robe sighed sadly, "I have to go."

"Go, my friend. I will ensure they will regret attacking on two fronts."

The frayed-robe vanished like the Black Knight did.

Flamboyant turned to face Vorbe, the vibrant colors of the outfit growing lighter and sharper.

"It's time."

Vorbe found himself in the altar room, the colorful individual before him pulling the stringed instrument into position.

Others appeared from the shadows, each with different styles of clothing and instruments, but all bards.

"For this kingdom," the flamboyant nodded to all the other bards, then focused on Vorbe, "We give this ultimate sacrifice."

Vorbe heard a new song, easily joining it with his instrument.

He felt a momentary connection to the land, its might gathering at the call of the song, weaving into the music as equal to them all.

On the last note, Vorbe looked at the flamboyant bard.

With a nod, the spell took his life.

A hand touched his wrist, jolting him as his body hit the floor.

His spirit turned, then blinked in confusion.

The flamboyant bard stood there.

"Come on," the bard smiled sadly, "I'll take you halfway."

Vorbe looked back, then winced as his body was seized up by the enemy, "Will they...?"

"No, they cannot claim your spirit. We both made sure once the spell was triggered, no necromancer could trap those who make this sacrifice."

Walking with the bard, he passed through the wall.

After a few seconds, they entered a large room.

Octave stood between crying children, healers ready to kill for their wards and the minotaurs leaning into a door, trying to strengthen the wood as it splintered.

Plodder trotted back and forth, barring teeth as his hooves clopped.

The flamboyant bard tugged on Vorbe's sleeve, "You can do no more for them."

Vorbe whispered to his oldest friend, "I hope someone else becomes your partner, Octave."

He continued on, but not before seeing Octave turn her head towards him, a questioning snort following him out of the keep.

Sinking deeper into the rock, Vorbe wondering if the Black Knight experienced traveling like this.

"Seems we were too good at our spells," a new voice drew Vorbe to his companion, then beyond to a newcomer.

He stared at the being before him in shock.

The frayed robes marked them as the same as the one he saw in his song.

Only the demonic features shouted they were something exotic.

"Its not everyday a demonic mage wages war with the help of a humble bard," the bard joked, "I have to return and direct the land to bury the invaders. Until the next time the spell is completed, friend."

The demonic mage looked at Vorbe, offered a clawed hand, "Let me regale you of my story, Master Bard Vorbe. The one where I faced a lich with the land I loved more than my own kind."

Vorbe blinked, "Your story is missing much."

"A demonic mage who was good at heart? Most would laugh you out of the inn for that tale. However, you'll want to learn this one. Shall we travel to the other side together?"

Vorbe nodded, settling his instrument at his side, "Yes."

Then he stepped side by side with the strongest elementalist of all time, listening to a wondrous tale.

One which would never be told among the living.

Chapter 28

Future

"[Chorus] Join the joy in our cycle"

Z'ronia turned her head back and forth, seeking sound, scent, or vibration.

It was as if all her senses were muted.

Then a beloved voice spoke clearly.

"It has been too long, Z'ronia."

Grella's voice filled her with happiness for a short breath.

Yet, there was something off about Grella.

Not truly her friend.

Z'ronia growled, "I do not take kindly to deceivers."

Time stretched to the breaking point before a different voice replied, "I did not mean offense. I wanted you to know you are in the company of allies."

"Who are you?" Z'ronia demanded.

A brush on her chest, on her very bones jolted her.

She didn't wear her armor. Where was it?

Then she knew who touched her.

"The Grasp," she bowed her head.

"Yes. The keeper of those who have ended their days of living, and the one who gives them back into life."

Z'ronia asked, "Why isn't Grella herself here?"

"She already forgot the person you knew her as. She returned to the living, a baby yet to be born."

Z'ronia ached as not meeting her friend again, "Our final goodbye was when she told me to leave."

A touch on her shoulder made her shiver with its similarity to Grella, yet not Grella, "She would not want you to grieve. Rejoice she will be experiencing a new life with the same courage and sense of justice as she rode with you. Though how long that will last is dependent on you."

Z'ronia rumbled, "I will not allow anyone to harm her."

"What of your love? She is here as well."

Horror filled Z'ronia.

She forgot Rathi could be called to vigil in her rush to arrive in time.

"No," Z'ronia clutched her shoulder, "I didn't mean to take Rathi as well."

"Would you return to the realm of the living to protect them?"

"How? The spell brought all undead to the other side to never return."

"The spell did the first part it intended to serve," the Grasp replied gently, "Only it was part of an ancient ceremony, bracketed by two spells. One where undead like yourself would come here to be judged. If they were fit to return to the living realm, they could if the caster had the strength to bring them back. Those unworthy would remain here for rest until the ceremony brought a new chance to go back."

Z'ronia shook her head, "I don't understand."

"The undead get additional time among the living as compared to a mortal, but they need to be worthy of it. Those like you must earn the right to remain. This spell is meant to bring all undead to be tested, then send them back home. The previous time this spell was used, the caster lost their ability to return, dooming all those who passed to be stuck here. However, you are the caster of this recent spell. Do you have the will to return to the living?"

Z'ronia pondered the question, her spirit torn in two different directions.

With Rathi here, possibly forever, L'pilth would be leaderless and without a guardian.

L'pilth was her home as well. Z'ronia wouldn't leave it unprotected when she could keep it safe and help them thrive. Hold it until a new king could rise.

No matter how her spirit ripped at leaving Rathi, taking the little the happiness she'd found, she couldn't leave her charges. The kingdom came first.

"I will return. Though," she halted.

"Though?" The Grasp prompted when she remained silent a while.

"I will not be able to stay there, alone. Without Rathi, I would be slowly worn down as water over rock. Eventually, I will be worn to nothing. I would come back to this side to be with her again," Z'ronia answered honestly, "By battle or this spell."

She got the impression the Grasp approved, though the grip on her shoulder didn't shift.

"Go with my blessing."

Z'ronia shifted, about to ask how, when a spell filled her mind, with the gentle voice of Grella explaining it to her.

This time she didn't mind as she recited the spell, grieving the lost of Rathi as she sought to return to the living realm.

She rose as she finished the spell.

Dorrick faded from her view as she found herself looking up at the sky, three of her pets pecking at her, as if attempting to wake her.

Standing, she looked where the demon army had marched.

Her magics swirled into her home, bringing her most powerful wards to bear.

While she may charge, her duty to the body remained.

Casting her spell to armor her pets, she readied her staves.

Stepping to sit on her biggest pet, she tugged at the woods to echo her next spell far and wide.

Then she yelled the command for her pets to take flight.

Her flock rose into the air, their cries rising in unison, wings pushing them into steep ascendents.

Looking out over the land, she grinned.

Small and large specks grew larger, rising to meet her pets.

Her army to fight a demon and her warriors.

As her army gathered, the land beneath shaded into darkness, then all sight was blocked.

Directing her pets towards their battle, she prayed the other lich stood strong.

War would ring across the land with their combined might.

Thus her charge began.

To victory or to defeat.

Epilogue
Ending

An exhausting year after the vigil for the Queen of Winter, Z'ronia rode Plodder back to Darksteel Keep.

Beside her, Octave carried a new rider: An undead bard, Master Bard Nilian, who proved a worthy companion on Z'ronia's travels.

His repertoire of songs eased the droll patrols and tasks of rebuilding L'pilth from the massive attack which happened while she was away.

The land carried the wounds in the form of new crags, rivers, sand pits and caverns. Yet those scars showed the land's victory over the enemy, and told the tale of Vorbe's sacrifice.

Escorting wagons full of trade goods up the path to the keep, she felt she'd finally come home.

Ghir'ali greeted them, "Any issues?"

"The other kingdoms did not contest our passage," Z'ronia dismounted.

"I learned a new song: The Battle for the Queen's Body," her companion chortled, "I will perform it for the King."

Leaving him to talk with Ghir'ali, Z'ronia walked with Plodder to the stable, making sure he was settled before entering the keep.

Stepping into the great hall, she walked to her normal listening spot, passing those making a feast ready.

"Black Knight," the Queen of Spring greeted, his voice warm to her tired ears.

"Queen of Spring," she replied, "Was your journey tranquil?"

"Absolutely," he laughed, "I must say traveling through the kingdoms south of this one proved much nicer since you wiped out the remaining liches."

"Master Bard Nilian is to thank for that accomplishment," she stated as said bard arrived, his voice rising and falling with a lively song he found in a distant tavern.

"Ah, Master Bard Nilian," the Queen moved away, "Will we have a song to celebrate our arrival?"

"I will recite the Battle for the Queen's Body. A bard was on the field when you held vigil for the Queen of Winter and they did an impressive job of it."

Z'ronia stepped to the side of the throne, stood at attention.

The touch on her elbow relaxed the tension in her shoulders.

Rathi's voice soothed her, "The caravan?"

"Arrived with all members intact," Z'ronia reported.

"Good. Once our guests retire for the evening, please come by. I have a new game we can play."

Z'ronia smiled, recalling the sound game Rathi played with her the week before, "Of course, King Rathi."

Then Master Bard Nilian began his song, his voice filling the hall, sending shivers down Z'ronia's spine as the events of that day drew her into the music.

Nilian relished his opportunity to bring the song to life, embellishing it with his skills to an audience of the living.

The song picked up after Z'ronia had dispatched the undead with her spell and the sidhe valiantly struggled against a demonic army.

"From the cave where the dead lay packed
Strode two fallen with ill-fated queen
Black armor gleaming as if newly forged

Besides a vampire thirsting for a drink
With a mighty voice the vampire challenged
While a deep tone seeped from dark armor
Magic swirled then a third joined them
Angelic magic sweeping back scorching heat
Then a storm burst from a point in clear sky
Rain dropping before becoming lances
Demonic visages twisted in anger and fear
Many falling before the three united in one
Battle waged across the field between heat and chill
Sidhe sliding in and out with eternal grace
Yet the demonic hordes marched forward
An endless mass constantly refreshed
Then from the sky dove Eclipse Hawks
Bringing another into battle with dual staves
A bellow burst the winter land into spring
Vines entwined with fiery enemies
Burrowing beneath armor as roots to stone
The battle looked to be won on their powers
When across the field a monstrosity rose
A demon lord bringing wildfires to the war
Driving back the valiant defenders
Evaporating the rain lances at clouds
Ashing vines back to blackened ground
Searing blood from bodies aplenty
Black armor summoned icy walls
Only for their formidable facades to melt
With manic laughter the demon called victory
Yet those embattled stood unyielding
Refusing inch by inch to give in easily
Despair filled the air as demonic creeped closer
Then earth began to rumble as if enraged

LICH EARS

An eerie horn sang across the land
Answered by voices ordained by war deities
On the horizon a colorful line crested
Cackling demons set to meet this new army
Only for ghostly apparitions to shoot into their midst
As deathly arrows from the Grasp's bow
Banshee cries rang in harmony with knightly charge
The first warriors clashing with demons
Each bearing glittering gem eyes full of power
Arrows, bolts, bolas, stones flew true
Undead of all types taking Grasp's will as writ
Noble kings easily recognized in their bearing
To hidden treasures of peasant lineage united
Rogues and thieves stealing weapons and lives
Mage, sorcerer, bard, paladin, cleric spells crossing
Druids taking animal forms undead as their norm
Chaos stole their chanted challenge at first
Yet as each strike bore down a demon it ran clearer
Black Knight, King Rathi
Those words stole strength from their foes
Many broke to flee from slaughter all around
Cut down by blade, arrow, mace or spell
Until the demon lord howled its defeat
Brought down by the Grasp's might
Silence echoed across battlefield as all turned
Facing the Black Knight and Kingly Vampire
While worn from nearly ceaseless struggles
Both carried an aura beyond regal and noble
There stood the chosen of the Grasp's fury
Embodying the one we all serve at our end
Victorious over all other tiffs we may have
Death reigns supreme and immutable

The two looked to the other then in one command
This legendary army of undeath parted ways
The command rings even now to my ears
Carrying an order to all of us, living and undead
Return to your duties until the Grasp calls you home"

As his voice died down, he looked around his audience, his mosaic mask keeping his ghostly nature hidden from view.

He watched those who listened to him shake off the lingering effects of the spelled song, then embraced their gratitude with aplomb.

Even his partner, the Black Knight, gave her appreciation, in her subtle way.

He began a new song, grateful the Grasp allowed him and all the others to return to the land of the living.

From the last remaining tomb guardian snatched in the area of the spell Z'ronia cast, to those who had waited millenniums for another to come get them with the spell, they all owed the lich standing beside the vampire everything.

Their community had been rebuilt with the will of one who'd only stepped out of her birthplace a few decades before.

At the urging of a mortal who could see beyond the surface to the wondrous spirit beneath the bones.

Miscellaneous Information About the World
Winter

- King - Male Gender, he/him pronouns
- Queen - Female Gender, she/her pronouns

Spring

- King - Male Gender, he/him pronouns
- Queen - Male Gender, he/him pronouns

Summer

- King - Female Gender, she/her pronouns
- Queen - Female Gender, she/her pronouns

Autumn

- King - Female Gender, she/her pronouns
- Queen - Male Gender, he/him pronouns

L'pilth

- King Rathi - Female Gender, primarily he/him pronouns, with some she/her depending on situation

- Black Knight / Z'ronia - Female Gender, primarily he/him pronouns, with some she/her depending on situation

About the Author

The author co-habitats with two rambunctious cats, one a tuxedo while the other is a grey tabby, and multiple, overburdened bookcases.

With twenty years of writing as a hobby, gleefully coaxing friends and family to review each new story, the author continues to add books to the collection for readers to enjoy.

To those authors starting their journeys: Mastering the craft of storytelling requires looking to past efforts as well as other authors to see better paths and skills. Continue improving, day by day. Your older works are stepping stones on the path you travel. Those early works will look worn as you have crossed over them many times to reach your newer works. Relish the lessons learned from the starting point, but don't let them weigh you down as you set out forward.

More information and blog posts can be found at:

ckmalavasic.com